TIGER STRIPED

SHIFTERS UNBOUND

JENNIFER ASHLEY

JA / AG PUBLISHING

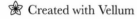

Shifters Unbound

(Paranormal Romance)

Pride Mates

Primal Bonds

Bodyguard

Wild Cat

Hard Mated

Mate Claimed

"Perfect Mate" (novella)

Lone Wolf

Tiger Magic

Feral Heat

Wild Wolf

Bear Attraction

Mate Bond

Lion Eyes

Bad Wolf

Wild Things

White Tiger

Guardian's Mate

Red Wolf

Midnight Wolf

Tiger Striped

(novella)

More to come!

Shifter Made ("Prequel" short story)

Immortals

(Paranormal Romance)

The Calling (by Jennifer Ashley)

The Darkening (by Robin Popp)

The Awakening (by Joy Nash)

The Gathering (by Jennifer Ashley)

The Redeeming (by Jennifer Ashley)

The Crossing (by Joy Nash)

The Haunting (by Robin Popp)

Blood Debt (by Joy Nash)

Wolf Hunt (by Jennifer Ashley)

Forbidden Taste (by Jennifer Ashley)

Stormwalker

(Paranormal Romance

w/a Allyson James)

Stormwalker

Firewalker

Shadow Walker

"Double Hexed"

Nightwalker

Dreamwalker

Dragon Bites

Riding Hard

(Contemporary Romance)

Adam

Grant

Carter

Tyler

Ross

Kyle

Ray

Snowbound in Starlight Bend

Historical Romances

The Mackenzies Series

The Madness of Lord Ian Mackenzie

Lady Isabella's Scandalous Marriage

The Many Sins of Lord Cameron

The Duke's Perfect Wife

A Mackenzie Family Christmas: The Perfect Gift

The Seduction of Elliot McBride

The Untamed Mackenzie

The Wicked Deeds of Daniel Mackenzie

Scandal and the Duchess

Rules for a Proper Governess

The Stolen Mackenzie Bride

A Mackenzie Clan Gathering

Alec Mackenzie's Art of Seduction

The Devilish Lord Will

CHAPTER ONE

Tiger woke in the night, knowing something was wrong in the world.

Carly, his mate, lay curled into his side, her wispy nightdress tickling his skin. Her golden-brown hair had escaped the ponytail she'd tucked it into, and silken strands brushed her face.

In his cubbyhole off their room, their son, Seth, slept in his crib, Tiger aware of his every breath. Seth had been born a human baby, as all half Shifter, half humans were, but his hair was tiger striped.

Carly was safe. Seth was safe. So why had Tiger come abruptly awake in the silence of the night?

He'd learned not to question what went on in his brain. Tiger wasn't like the other Shifters of this Shiftertown—he'd been born in a lab, the experiment of genetic engineers who'd really needed something better to do with their time.

Twenty-two of their experiments had failed. *Failed* meant the Shifters had died.

Number Twenty-Three was Tiger. The researchers had abandoned him when the lab shut down, and Tiger had existed in isolation for many years.

Now he lived here, he reminded himself, as he brushed his fingertips over Carly's soft skin. In a huge room at the top of a cozy bungalow that had been partitioned into two once Seth arrived. Tiger had a mate who loved him, and a cub of his own, two things he'd never truly believed would happen to him. The rest of this house was taken up with Liam Morrissey's family—Liam's mate and cub and his nephew, who'd welcomed Tiger into their home and made him one of their clan.

The window was open, but the night was quiet—as quiet as it ever got in Austin, near Mueller, the old airport. Tiger heard cars on the distant freeway, the drone of a low-flying heli-copter, someone laughing far away.

He heard Shifters as well, the nocturnal Felines who liked to prowl Shiftertown in the warmth of the September night. They hung out, went for runs under the stars, had sex in the shadows.

None of that had woken him. *Tiger can sleep through a tornado if he wants to*, Carly always said, flashing her big smile. She knew that for a fact.

Rapid thoughts ran through Tiger's head along with the brief, weird stream of numbers he sometimes saw in the back of his brain. Tiger didn't know what the numbers meant or where they came from. He only knew they oriented him to things he needed to understand or situa-tions no one but him could handle.

The uneasy silence was broken by sudden, intense screams. All-out, boiling-in-hell, please-help-me screaming. It filled Tiger's brain and blotted out everything—the house, his cub, Carly and her soothing touch.

Wordless. Terrified. In so much torment.

Tiger slammed his hands to his head, squeezing to make the pain and fear cease, but they wouldn't be silenced.

Carly and Seth slept on, oblivious, because

the sound wasn't here, in the air around them. It was inside Tiger's mind.

From far, far away, a being cried out, and Tiger heard.

Search and rescue.

Tiger had been made for it—his original purpose. Subsequent researchers had changed their tactics and tried to transform him into a super fighter, a living machine, but his idealistic, first creators had wanted to use Tiger to find people lost and on their last hope.

During the past year, Shifter Bureau had called on Tiger to locate stranded hikers, lost cubs, and the occasional criminal eluding the human police. Tiger had tapped into his abilities and found them, but it had never been like this.

Not this invading mind-pounding agony, a desperation that tore into Tiger's psyche.

He had to find the being in trouble. *Now.*

Tiger rose in silence, pulled on his clothes, and left the house.

CARLY WOKE AS SOON AS THEIR BEDROOM door shut. She sat up, pushing her hair from her eyes, and looked around the moonlit room. Tiger was gone.

Seth snoozed happily in his crib beyond the open door to his tiny bedroom. Mothers envied Carly, because Seth had been a good sleeper from day one, and a happy baby. He seemed to know that his father, the indestructible Tiger, would let nothing bad happen to him. Which was true.

But sometimes Tiger would go *remote*, listening to voices Carly couldn't hear. Or he'd simply walk out without a word, like tonight. She always sensed when he disappeared from the bed, her connection to him knowing his agitation.

Carly rose, pulled on a robe, and checked Seth in his crib. He lay on his stomach, his orange and black hair sticking up every which way, his back rising and falling in contented sleep.

Carly adjusted his blanket and tiptoed out.

She reached the stairs to see Tiger come off the last step and make for the front door. He was fully dressed, his muscles hard under the black T-shirt he'd snatched up to go with his jeans.

Carly ran after him. She didn't want to wake

the rest of the house by calling his name, but she knew that if she didn't stop him, he'd vanish. The last time this had happened, he'd walked into Faerie via a house in New Orleans into terrible danger. When Carly had finally pried the details of *that* story from him, he'd looked at her as though he didn't understand why she'd been worried.

Wherever he was heading this time, she was going with him. Mates protected each other, and she wasn't about to lose Tiger to a bunch of mean-ass Fae, or Shifters, or humans, or whatever enemy he'd find this time.

By the time Carly exited the house, Tiger was on the driveway next door, looking over Dylan Morrissey's small white pickup as though trying to figure out the mystery of it. Cool air touched Carly through her thin robe as she moved carefully on her bare feet across the thin strip of grass that separated the driveways.

She made it to the truck and rested her hands on its cool hood. "Where are you going, Tiger?" she asked softly.

Tiger at last swung to look at her, and Carly took a stunned step back.

His golden eyes were wide with pain and

shock, his black and orange hair pulled awry as though he'd been tearing at it.

Carly's heart beat faster. "Tiger?"

Tiger balled his huge fists. "I have to go." His voice cracked like he'd swallowed dust.

"Go where? Back to Faerie?"

Tiger looked puzzled. "No. Somewhere in the human world."

"Sweetie, could you narrow that down just a *little* bit?" Carly lifted her thumb and forefinger in demonstration.

Tiger gazed around the dark street, old-growth trees casting deeper shadows on the early twentieth-century bungalows. "No," he answered.

"So, what's your plan? Hot-wire Dylan's truck and drive off somewhere in the human world? And I can't believe I'm standing here talking about worlds, like there really is more than one."

"There are an infinite number," Tiger said, but Carly could tell he wasn't interested in discussing quantum physics right now.

"You can't just ask Dylan for the keys? Or for me to take you? Or Connor? You know he's always up for adventure, anytime of the day or night."

Tiger continued to eye the truck, occasionally running a hand through his hair, rumpling it
further. Carly realized he wasn't really hearing
her, but listening to the something inside his
mind. He did that sometimes.

She put one hand on her hip. "You know,
other women might get the wrong idea
watching their husband sneak off in the middle
of the night."

Tiger glanced at her. "Why?"

"Because she'd think he was sleeping around
on her, silly."

That got his attention. Tiger stared at Carly
in amazement. "You are my mate." As though
the statement said it all.

"Well, that's a relief. In that case, let me get
dressed and drive you. A question—is it safer to
leave Seth at home with a babysitter or to bring
him with us?"

Tiger scowled at her, a flicker of his usual
self showing through his glassy-eyed distraction.
"Seth will stay home. So will you."

"Not a chance, honey." Carly pointed at
him. "Don't you go anywhere for a sec,
all right?"

Carly turned and fled back into the house
and up the stairs to their bedroom. She tore off

the robe and cute nighty Kim had bought her for her last birthday, and grabbed clothes and flung them on. She ended up in one of Tiger's huge T-shirts, a pair of her own denim shorts, and sandals. Carly scraped her hair into a ponytail and caught up her son, who opened one sleepy eye and snuggled into her.

Carly's heart throbbed with a sudden ache. She had Tiger and Seth, was as happy as she'd ever been.

She was going after Tiger tonight to make sure they all *stayed* a happy family. Tiger walked into dangerous crap all the time—mostly because other Shifters went too far, and Tiger had to rush in and save them.

Carly was tired of it. His search-and-rescue missions to help people were one thing. Other Shifters getting him into perilous battles, especially with the scary Fae, was something else.

She put Seth into his carrier, crept down the stairs with him, and stealthily entered the bedroom Kim shared with her mate Liam and their baby daughter.

Carly tried to move as softly as she could, though she knew she'd never be quiet enough to escape a Shifter's notice, but she saw that tonight it didn't matter. Liam wasn't in the bed.

Kim was alone, sleeping soundly, one arm flung across the pillow where Liam was supposed to be.

Katriona, their two-year-old daughter, was curled up in her small bed with bumpers on the sides. Carly set Seth, still sleeping, on the wide, low dresser next to the bed, where Kim would see him as soon as she woke.

She didn't want to leave Seth—everything in her cried out not to—but she knew he would be safe here with Kim and Liam. Tiger, if he raced out into the world, wouldn't be.

Carly kissed Seth's forehead and hurried from the room.

She saw why Liam wasn't in his bed as soon as she made it out the door, baggy purse in hand. Liam gazed across the hood of his father's truck at Tiger, and Tiger scowled back at him.

"I'm supposed to be taking care of you, lad," Carly heard Liam say.

Liam Morrissey, the leader of this Shiftertown, a dark-haired, blue-eyed man who changed into black-maned lion when he was so inclined, was trying to outstare Tiger. He'd been leading the Shiftertown for about three years now, usually in a laid-back way, but when he asserted his authority, everyone took notice.

Tiger wasn't answering, a bad sign. Tiger too could be laid-back to the point of comatose, not really minding that cubs crawled all over him or other Shifters used his incredible strength for everything from opening jars to battling insane Fae warriors.

Usually Tiger shrugged, opened the jar, destroyed the warriors, and went back to lounging on the porch with Carly, Seth in his arms.

Tonight Tiger snarled as Liam took a step toward him. Liam held up his hands in a placating manner, but Tiger's warning growls only increased.

"It's all right," Carly said quickly to Liam. "I'm going with him, whatever he's off to do."

Tiger snapped his focus to her, his eyes a hot yellow. "No, you are *not.*"

Carly folded her arms, her purse banging against her side. "Yes, I am. You're in no shape to drive this thing. Besides if I steal Dylan's pickup, you'll have to protect me from him once we get back."

She finished her declaration, scooted around Tiger before Tiger could gather himself to stop her, and slid into the driver's seat. No need to hot-wire the truck, she saw once she was behind the wheel. Dylan had left his keys in the ignition.

Carly shut the door and leaned out the window to Tiger. "Are you coming?"

Tiger stared down at her a moment, and then he jolted to life, making his silent and swift way around to the passenger door and into the truck. Carly smiled at Liam as he glared at them both.

"I'll bring him back in one piece," she said, starting the ignition. "Promise."

"It's past curfew," Liam tried. "If he's caught …"

… out of Shiftertown in the middle of the night, humans wouldn't hesitate to arrest Tiger, cage him, put him on trial, execute him, or at least return him to a lab to be studied, maybe forever.

Carly reached over and unlocked the Collar from around Tiger's neck. Collars were designed to deeply shock the Shifter who grew violent, and it was against the law to remove them.

Tiger's Collar, though, was fake. When he'd been rescued from Area 51 and brought to live in this Shiftertown it was decided that Tiger wouldn't have to wear a real Collar. The Collars went on painfully, and Tiger was … well, Tiger. After an aborted attempt, no one else was brave enough to try to put a true one around his neck.

She dropped the black and silver chain into Tiger's hand. Tiger looked like a Shifter no matter what—large, strong, fierce—and that was when he sat still. But without the Collar, it might take humans a few minutes to figure out what he was, and by that time they could be gone.

Carly called through the open window to Liam, "Tell Kim I owe her one, and that we'll be back soon. Buh-bye."

She gave him a cheery wave, disguising her qualms. Tiger had gone off before, yes, even in the middle of the night, but not like this. Not with this—*obsession*. She hadn't worried about him like this those other times. This was different.

Carly backed the truck from the driveway and out into the dark street. A single light glowed at the end of the block—Shifters preferred the shadows.

Liam watched them go, folding his arms over his broad chest. He didn't run after them or yell or try to alert his father that Carly and Tiger were taking off in his truck.

Carly wondered *why* he was letting them go so easily. Liam was crafty, always having about twenty-seven plans up his sleeve. Liam simply backing off didn't bode well, but Tiger was undeterred.

Very few roads led out of Shiftertown. When Carly reached the corner of the main street, next to a vacant lot, she asked, "Which way?"

Tiger pointed to the left. No hesitation. He had his eyes closed, his head back, not even bothering to look. He was trusting that she'd take him where he needed to go and bring him home safely.

It was Carly who paused uncertainly. If she drove Tiger away from Shiftertown, could she protect him? At home, even with all the restrictions put on Shifters, Tiger was surrounded by powerful friends who would help him and run interference for him with Shifter Bureau. Out in the world, though …

"He wants you to take a left," said a male voice behind her.

Carly shrieked, coming three inches off the seat before she plopped back down.

A young man rose from the bed of the truck to peer in through the cab's back window. He was muffled in a hoodie zipped up to his chin, but the dark hair of his uncles and grandfather peeped from under the hood, and Morrissey blue eyes gazed at her.

"Go on, Carly," Connor Morrissey said in a voice that had deepened in the last year, the trace of Irish keeping it soft. "Before Uncle Liam figures out I'm with you. Hurry!"

CHAPTER TWO

Tiger popped his eyes open and looked back to see Connor grab the window ledge as Carly stepped on the gas and rounded the corner.

Connor was a cub by Shifter standards, and Tiger's first priority in his world, after loving and taking care of Carly and Seth, was to protect cubs.

Tiger rapidly weighed the pros and cons of turning around to take Connor home versus looking after him. He couldn't take Connor into danger.

But then the screaming in his head escalated, begging wordlessly for him to hurry. Tiger chose.

"Stay close to me," he told Connor. "No fighting."

Carly slammed on the brakes for a red light. "Exactly. You are going to get me into so much trouble, Connor. What are you doing hiding in the back of Dylan's truck?"

"Couldn't sleep in the house," Connor said without concern. "Too hot. And Uncle Liam and I had a row."

A *row* meant an argument. A word Tiger had learned since he'd come to live with the Morrisseys.

"What about this time?" Carly asked. She sped off when the traffic light glowed green. "No, don't tell me. You wanted to go to the fight club again."

"I could kick the ass of any Shifter put in front of me." Connor's confidence radiated from him. "Okay, maybe except Spike. Or Ronan. But pretty much everyone else. I don't understand why I have to wait until my Transition."

Tiger closed his eyes. The Transition from cubhood to adulthood, which usually happened when a cub was in his twenties, meant restlessness, quick anger, the need to fight, and later, the urgent need to mate. Tiger's had been unbelievably painful and terrifying, hell to remember.

The stream of numbers in front of his eyeballs that appeared when he closed his eyes was hard to take, and he opened his eyes again.

"You're a cub," he said to Connor. "Against the fight club rules. They won't change them for you."

"Since when did *you* follow the rules? Witness—you're out running around Austin with a delinquent cub in the middle of the night. Where are we going?" Connor sounded interested, not worried.

"That way," Tiger said, pointing straight ahead of them.

"I'm hoping it isn't far," Carly said. "And that Tiger will tell me when we get there."

"I don't know how far." Tiger slid his hand across the seat and rested it on Carly's thigh. Touching her eased the pain a little.

Another term Tiger had learned since coming to live with the Morrisseys was *unconditional love*. He hadn't understood what it meant until he'd met Carly.

"Someone needs me. I think." He'd felt people calling out to him before, but tonight's cry for help seemed to blossom from the base of his brain.

Carly flashed him a tight smile. "The joy of being Tiger."

"Huh," Connor said. He watched Carly drive for another moment or two, and then settled down into the pickup's bed and buried himself under a blanket.

"You okay?" Carly asked Tiger in a quiet voice.

Tiger had no idea. In his search-and-rescue missions, supervised by Walker Danielson, the liaison between the Austin Shiftertown and Shifter Bureau, he'd helped find missing hikers in the Sierras, a small craft lost at sea with all the crew aboard, children in and around the Austin area who'd either wandered away from their parents or been taken, and two men wanted for a robbery turned violent.

On those missions, Walker had told Tiger about the missing people, and they'd started the search in their last known location. Tiger had tracked them from there.

This time, Tiger only had a pull, a knowledge that *someone* out in the world was in great danger.

Carly continued driving south. They crossed

Boggy Creek, then the river. Traffic was at a minimum, most bars and restaurants closed this late, the business people who hit their offices on the dot of eight not yet awake.

Roads merged and Carly glanced questioningly at Tiger. He said nothing until they reached what Carly called a mix-master, and he pointed west. "That way."

Carly swung into the lane under the sign that read "Ben White Blvd." That road ran west through Austin, and Tiger relaxed. This was right.

Lights of all-night restaurants broke the darkness, and Tiger realized he was hungry. But they couldn't stop. Not yet.

When Ben White intersected with the freeway, Carly looked at Tiger again, but he gestured her to keep straight on. In the truck bed, hidden by the blankets, Connor settled into slumber—Tiger could sense his deep and even breathing.

"I'm going to need a good story to tell Dylan, you know," Carly said as she drove through the darkness. "And Liam. But mostly Dylan, for taking his truck."

Tiger liked Carly's voice, the soft syllables of her Texas accent rippling pleasant sensations through him. He'd liked her voice from the moment she'd called out to him from the side of the highway where her car had broken down. She'd been wearing a white dress and sunglasses, her hair in what she called a French braid, one hand on her hip, very annoyed at the car that had stalled on her.

He'd liked other things about her too, her tight, curvy body, her hair he wanted to nuzzle, and most especially her eyes. They were green with flecks of gray, and had looked straight into his without fear.

Tiger had been knocked over by her that day and he hadn't yet recovered.

"We'll tell Dylan the truth," Tiger answered her. "Whenever we know it."

Carly let out an exasperated breath but continued to drive.

They left the lights of Austin behind and moved through developing suburbs toward Dripping Springs and then beyond. At the T junction of the 290 and 281, Tiger felt the pull north, and Carly turned that way, heading toward Johnson City.

They were getting close to the sprawling ranch that housed a secret enclave of Shifters, where Kendrick the white tiger kept his un-

Collared Shifters off the human radar. Tiger wondered whether he was feeling one of Kendrick's Shifters, but at the turnoff, Tiger knew this wasn't the case. He needed to keep moving west.

Past Johnson City, Carly tried to make conversation. "Did you know there were a lot of vintners out here?" She pointed to a sign under a clump of trees, barely visible in her headlights. "And around Fredericksburg. Kim and I talked about doing a wine tour, but now we have babies, which means we're busy. Even Yvette likes trying their wines, and you know what a foodie she is."

Yvette, former Parisian model, owned an art gallery with her husband who'd once been her photographer. Yvette and Armand were Carly's former employers and now close friends. They loved cooking and inviting people over to enjoy the food. They were Tiger's friends too, he realized. Humans who accepted him.

He turned the thought over in his mind, the part that wasn't preoccupied with whoever was calling out to him, finding this fact interesting and pleasant.

He didn't answer Carly, but she was used to that. She could talk enough for both of them.

They went through Fredericksburg's dark streets, which had, Carly said, an Old West feel and restored Victorian homes. Connor slept silently in the back, never waking as they sped onward.

When the road dead-ended at the I-10, Tiger waved for Carly to merge onto the westbound lane, Carly's headlights cutting the darkness. They were the only car on the road at this early hour.

"Do you remember the last time we drove out this way?" Carly asked after a while. "I ended up meeting you in the middle-of-nowhere Mexico. Not going there again, I hope?"

Tiger considered and shook his head. "I don't think so."

"Well," Carly continued breezily. "That's good to know."

He should apologize, he thought. Tiger had dragged his mate out in the middle of the night to drive across flat, dry, empty land, and he couldn't tell her why, or where.

Carly had insisted on coming, yes, but Tiger could have stopped her, and he knew it. He could have carried her back into the house or thrust her at Liam and jumped into the truck and sped off.

Then he would have wrecked the truck, because Carly was right. He wasn't good at driving enclosed vehicles. Motorcycles, yes— Connor and Sean, Liam's brother, had taught him. Cars and pickups he hadn't learned the hang of. He could fix any automobile he touched, but driving was different.

The sun rose, revealing, as Carly might say, *a whole lotta nothing*. Two lanes of freeway, one heading east, one west, were divided by a strip of dust and dried grass. More dried grasses and dust filled the sides of the road as far as Tiger could see. A long way in the distance the bump of a craggy mountain hovered on the horizon.

There was movement in the back. Blankets parted and Connor emerged, his hoodie still firmly fastened over his Collar.

"Where the hell are we?" he mumbled, blinking blearily.

"Somewhere between Fort Stockton and El Paso," Carly answered. "You want to drive, Connor? I'm getting tired."

Tiger instantly came alert. "Are you?"

Carly slanted him a glance. "Hmm, let's see —I woke up at three in the morning and stole a truck, and now I'm in the middle of West Texas watching the sun come up behind me. I'd say I'm a little tired, sweetie."

She'd said nothing, Tiger understood, because Carly always wanted to appear strong for him. She'd been like that the months she'd been pregnant, even when she'd gone into labor.

Tiger wasn't exactly sure why Carly wanted to show Tiger her resilience, and it troubled him when he pushed her too hard and didn't realize it.

"Drive, Connor," he commanded.

"Sure thing." Connor now sounded perfectly alert—Shifters could wake up fast. "Rest area ahead," he said, pointing at a blue sign they zoomed toward.

Carly pulled off the road and into the long drive that wound around picnic tables, vending machines, and a block of bathrooms. A few other cars had parked, their drivers taking breaks. Folks wandered around the parking area, gazing out at the empty land, or they leaned against their vehicle, fingers curled around a cup of coffee.

The human travelers cast curious glances at the three getting out of the truck—Tiger with his bulk followed by a beautiful woman in a baggy T-shirt and shorts, Connor leaping from the bed of the truck with young ease.

Carly mumbled something about the bathroom and hurried up the concrete path. Tiger walked after her, planting himself just outside the bathroom door. He'd learned enough about the human world not to charge in after her, but if Carly called for help, he'd be right there.

Female travelers eyed Tiger nervously as they slid around him to get to the bathroom, but he couldn't make himself move. Carly came out again in a short time, not surprised to find him two feet from the door. She only smiled at him, took his hand, and walked with him back to the truck.

Connor was already in the driver's seat. He had the radio on, and was singing to a lively tune.

Carly climbed in between Connor and Tiger, and they rolled out again. Tiger liked his mate beside him, where she brushed against him whenever she moved. She could rest her head on his shoulder and sleep if she wanted to.

At the moment, she was singing with Connor, the two of them harmonizing on a country song. Tiger could dissect the music and talk about it, but he couldn't catch the rhythm and find the joy of it like Carly. She bounced on the seat as she danced to the quick beat, banging warmly into Tiger.

When the song finished, Carly laughed, and she and Connor high-fived. Carly then snuggled back into Tiger and let out a tired sigh.

The comfort of her leaked through Tiger's distress. Her hair smelled of jasmine, her skin of soap and sleep. Tiger closed his arms around her, resting his forehead on her sleek hair. She smelled of Tiger as well, the scent mark he'd breathed on her the first day they'd met.

Carly, humming along with the next song, turned to press a kiss to Tiger's cheek, her lips petal soft.

"Thought so." Connor's voice cut through the quiet peace Tiger had finally managed to find.

Connor was studying the rearview mirror, darting glances ahead to adjust the wheel before returning his stare to the mirror.

Carly's T-shirt rustled as she pushed herself upright. "What is it?"

"Someone's following us." Connor punched the button to turn off the radio, the sudden silence jarring. "They've been with us for a while."

Carly gave him a skeptical look. "Don't
know if you've noticed, but there's only one
road out here, the one we're on. Where else are
they going to go?"

"They hang back and don't pass," Connor
said. "They slow down when there's a chance of
catching up." He checked the mirror. "I saw
them behind us before we stopped. And now
they're right back there again. Coincidence?"

"Could be." Carly made a show of glancing
at the open and empty desert. "One rest area in
fifty miles, no real towns for the next, oh,
hundred or so. So they stopped in the same rest
area we did. What are the odds?"

"Don't make fun," Connor said without
offense. "I didn't see them in the rest area, so
they were staying out of sight on purpose."

"All right, you might have a point." Carly
turned to glance out the back window. "You
think it's Liam, making sure you both are okay?
Or Shifter Bureau coming after you for breaking
curfew?"

Tiger unrolled the passenger window and
moved the mirror on his side to see behind
them. The cool of the morning flowed into the
cab, as well as the noise of air rushing past at
eighty miles an hour.

Tiger focused on the black vehicle about a mile behind them, his instincts and the numbers in his brain calculating who they could be and why they were following. He drew and dismissed several conclusions in rapid succession.

"It's not Liam," Tiger said firmly. "Not Dylan either. And not Shifter Bureau."

"Who then?" Connor asked in bewilderment.

"Not sure." Tiger frowned. It should bother him that he didn't know, but the anguish pounding at him kept him from focusing.

Connor huffed. "I don't like that. If *Tiger* doesn't know what's going on, then we're screwed."

"Not necessarily," Carly said quickly. "It might be someone helpful."

She always tried to look at the bright side, his mate. Although, Tiger conceded, she was happy to take action when she was wrong. Carly was a fighter, even if she used the weapons of smiles and quiet fierceness to make her point.

"With two runaway Shifters who are heading out of their state?" Connor asked. "One without a Collar? Breaking all kinds of rules? Nope, we're screwed."

Carly twisted to look behind them again, her

hair brushing Tiger's cheek. "Try and lose them," she told Connor.

"There is nowhere to lose them," Tiger pointed out.

"Oh yeah?" Connor said, a grin spreading across his face. "We'll see about that."

He stomped on the accelerator and the truck leapt forward, dust on the road swirling to lift high in their wake.

CHAPTER THREE

The pickup rattled and protested as Connor pushed the speedometer to ninety, the old truck not built to take the momentum.

The engine hummed along fine—Shifters kept their vehicles in top condition. The chassis, however, rattled and groaned, threatening to shatter at any moment. Carly worried less about being stranded in the middle of West Texas with no water than she did about explaining to Dylan that they'd destroyed his pickup.

Tiger leaned against the corner of the seat, eyes closed as though trusting Connor to take them to safety. Carly wished she could be so unruffled.

She peered anxiously behind them and breathed a little easier when she saw that the black SUV had dropped back.

Connor kept up the speed, overtaking an eighteen-wheeler, waving cheerfully at the driver as they went by. The driver sounded his horn back in playful response. Must be nice to be so chipper in the morning.

While they were now well ahead of the pursuing vehicle, Carly didn't relax completely. There were few turnoffs here, and those they passed, like the road to Marfa, were narrow and not well trafficked. Anyone chasing them for a nefarious purpose had a better chance of cornering them on a smaller road and stranding them, or worse.

Their best option was to go into El Paso, where they could lose a pursuit on busy streets or by hiding out in a packed parking lot. They'd have the opportunity to change vehicles if necessary too, though Carly cringed as she imagined explaining *that* to Dylan.

They could always mail him his keys with a note, she supposed. And then change their names and flee the country.

Connor continued down the freeway, the speedometer steady at ninety. Carly's new worry was that there'd be a cop lurking at the side of the road waiting to bust them. There were no handy trees for a patrol car to hide behind, but the dry land had dips and depressions, and a local officer would know the best ones to use as blinds.

"You can probably back off a little, Connor," she said nervously. "If you're pulled over and they find out you two are Shifters …"

"There aren't any police." Tiger's words vibrated through her. "Not for a long way."

Connor glanced at Tiger but said nothing. Carly didn't question him. Even after a year of living with Tiger she wasn't sure *how* he knew the things he knew. But he did, and he was never wrong.

The mountains on the horizon drew nearer and resolved into tall, dry peaks that, according to the map on Carly's phone, marched down to the canyons around the Rio Grande. The freeway rolled on to the farthest western tip of Texas, the border with Mexico now only a few miles to the south.

As the day grew bright and hot, the traffic picked up, and a city glittered ahead of them. Connor had to slow at last, and they followed a stream of cars into the spread of El Paso.

The I-10 went through the outskirts of the city and into downtown, the sprawl of Juarez paralleling them across the river. Carly expected Tiger to sit up and point the way, or at least open his eyes, but he continued to lounge against the door, as quiet as he'd been on the open road.

"Tiger?" Carly's alarm grew when she saw that his eyes were half open, his golden irises glassy. "Tiger!"

Tiger did a slow blink, as though bringing himself back from whatever distant place he'd been. His face softened. "Carly."

"You all right?" Carly twined one hand through his and rubbed the backs of his fingers. "Are we going the right way?"

Tiger stared out the window. "Yes," he said after a moment.

Connor clutched the wheel, concentrating on the road and the stream of cars, SUVs, trucks, and motorcycles surrounding them. "We need gas."

"There's a place." Carly pointed to an exit whose ramp ran up onto a hill.

Connor swiftly navigated to the exit and followed a line of cars to the intersection above, pulling into the gas station and parking in front of a pump. He started to get out, but Carly tugged him back.

"Let me," she said. "You guys keep a low profile."

As low a profile as two hard-bodied men, one burying himself in a hoodie and one with black-and-orange striped hair, could keep.

Carly had to climb over Tiger, pressing her hand to his chest to keep him from getting out with her. She paused as she slid across his lap, lowering her head to kiss him.

Tiger's eyes flickered, the pain she saw inside them easing a bit. Carly touched his face.

"We'll find whoever you're looking for," she whispered. "Promise."

Tiger slid one strong hand behind her neck and pulled her to him for a deeper kiss.

Tiger's heart was rocketing, thudding hard behind his T-shirt, his skin roasting. Even so, Tiger's kiss opened Carly's mouth and let her taste him, the joy of being with him embracing her. They'd made love last night before they'd fallen asleep, and the heat of that filled Carly once more.

Connor cleared his throat. "Any day," he said, his voice cracking with worry. "Can you two do your spooning once we're on the road again?"

Tiger gently lifted Carly from him, opened the door, and set her down on her feet outside. He sent her a regretful look as Carly steadied herself on the pavement, the smell of hot asphalt and warm gas fumes filling the air.

It was September, but they were now officially in the Southwest, where triple-digit temperatures lingered until late autumn. The lot's heat came through the soles of Carly's sandals, making her toes curl.

Carly took out her credit card to slide into the pump's reader, and then reconsidered. If Tiger had been reported at large, Shifter Bureau might try to trace him through her purchases. They'd guess or learn Carly was with him.

She tucked the card away and hurried into the convenience store, where she paid cash for the gas, giving the clerk a warm smile.

Her wallet was depressingly empty. They'd have to get more money soon, from somewhere. No telling how long this road trip would be. But pursuers could trace her through ATM withdrawals as well. Cutting-edge technology had put the world into a goldfish bowl.

Carly purchased some water and low-cost

snacks, and trotted with everything back to the car. She thrust the bag of goodies through the open window at Tiger then wrestled the nozzle from the pump and into the pickup's tank.

A man on the other side of the pump glanced over, then looked indignant when he saw Carly filling the tank while two men lazed on their asses in the truck. Carly gave the man a bright smile.

"I insist," she said.

The man gave her a little nod in return, the *Whatever* loud and clear. He finished, started his car, and drove away.

As Carly watched the numbers on the pump move with agonizing slowness, Connor popped open the front door and slid out of the cab.

"Where are *you* going?" Carly demanded.

"I have to pee." Connor zipped the hoodie more securely over his Collar, thrust his hands into his pockets, and slunk into the convenience store.

Carly had used the bathroom at the rest area, but that had been an hour or so ago, and agitation wasn't helping. The restroom sounded like a good idea. She hung up the nozzle, closed the gas tank, and walked around the truck to Tiger. "Don't go anywhere," she said.

He opened his eyes, his protective look returning. Carly put her hand on his arm.

"Seriously don't," she said quickly. "I'm just going to the bathroom, and Connor's in there. We're all safer if you don't draw attention."

Carly saw Tiger acknowledge this, but he didn't like it. She patted the back of his hand. "Next time you flee town, steal a big RV with a working bathroom."

Tiger nodded in all seriousness. "I will."

Carly raced into the store, feeling Tiger watch her all the way. She smiled at the clerk again and ducked into the back, following the "Restrooms" sign. She heard water running in the men's room and hoped Connor would get back out to the truck soon to keep an eye on Tiger.

She dashed into the empty women's room and a mostly clean stall with some relief. A few minutes later, she was at the sink, scrubbing her hands and splashing water on her face.

The blotchy mirror showed that she looked awful. Hanks of honey brown hair framed her face, her Scrunchie hanging on by one strand. Her cheeks were pale, shadows like bruises beneath her eyes.

Carly pulled off the Scrunchie, patted water

onto her hair, and tried to tame it into a neater ponytail. She grabbed paper towels, dried her hands and face, and sprinted out, doing a two-point slam-dunk of the paper towels into the trash can.

She reached the front door of the convenience store in time to hear Connor shout. Her heart dropped when she saw a black SUV with dark windows gleaming in the bright sunlight pull in behind the pickup and four men in black fatigues leap out.

Connor had apparently lingered in the store to buy another handful of candy bars. Now he halted outside the door, his mouth open from his cry of warning.

Tiger was in the pickup's driver's seat. He had the engine started, and as Carly watched, the small truck leapt forward, tires squealing, and bolted out of the lot.

CHAPTER FOUR

Connor grabbed Carly's wrist. She managed a squeak of surprise before Connor dragged her in the opposite direction from the SUV.

Two of the men in black saw them and started after them, but Connor, a lion Shifter at the peak of his youth, could *run*.

Carly had to pump her legs hard to keep up with him. Connor raced with her around to the back of the gas station just as Dylan's pickup careened around the corner into the narrow road behind it.

The pickup slowed a fraction, and Connor slung his arm firmly around Carly and sprang with her into the bed of the moving truck.

"Whoop!" Carly landed hard on Connor, both of them sliding rearward as Tiger sped up. Carly's feet slammed into the tailgate, and she and Connor held on to each other as the truck spun around another corner and down the street.

As soon as she was able, Carly untangled herself from Connor and pulled herself up to look over the tailgate. They were racing away from the gas station, heading for the ramp to the freeway. The men in black dove into the SUV, the vehicle already moving.

An eighteen-wheeler chose that moment to rumble slowly past the station, blocking the exit. Carly saw the black vehicle come to a sudden halt, and then frantically reverse, looking for another way out.

Carly held up both fists. "Eat that, suckers!"

Tiger careened around cars, and Carly lost sight of the SUV. She collapsed into the truck's bed to find Connor glaring at her.

"Never taunt Shifter Bureau agents," he said. "It only gets you into trouble. Trust me."

"Tiger said they weren't Shifter Bureau. That is, if those were the same guys following us on the freeway."

"Oh, they're the same ones," Connor answered darkly. "And Tiger could be wrong."

Carly laughed. "Tiger's never wrong, honey. If says they aren't Shifter Bureau, then they're not."

Tiger swung the truck through a contingent of bikers on the entrance ramp and roared onto the freeway. The roadway was crowded, the city awake and moving. Tiger slipped and slid through traffic, completely putting the lie to his claim that he had a hard time driving anything but motorcycles.

Carly pulled herself up painfully to look into the cab, the wind destroying the ponytail she'd painstakingly redone in the bathroom.

She sucked in a sharp breath. Tiger was driving all right, zipping and zigging through cars, SUVs, pickups, semis, motorcycles … with his eyes closed.

Carly opened her mouth to cry out, then thought better of it. Tiger was following the curve of the lanes, moving around other vehicles with ease, adjusting to the traffic as though on autopilot. Startling him right now might be deadly.

Tiger had told Carly that sometimes he saw

faint streams of numbers, like computer commands, scrolling through the back of his mind. Carly often wondered whether the researchers from Area 51 had stuck some kind of chip inside him, but Tiger didn't know.

In any case, Tiger was driving the truck steadily along, leaving the black SUV far behind.

Carly knew the reprieve was temporary. Traffic was already thinning as they reached the edge of town, and the road beyond would empty. The SUV would easily catch up with them there.

They sped out of the city limits and passed a sign that read *Welcome to New Mexico, Land of Enchantment.*

Carly hunkered down with Connor, pulling the fleece blankets he'd been curled up in over them both. The sun was hot but the wind was cool, and hiding from the blaring desert sun was always a good idea.

"Where are we?" Connor asked under the dim confines of the blankets.

"New Mexico." Carly swallowed. "I wonder if he's heading all the way to the coast. Will we have to jump aboard a ship?"

Connor only shrugged, curled up and closed his eyes.

He didn't worry about much, did Connor, Carly thought with envy. He was an amazing young man, chafing at the overprotectiveness of his uncles and grandfather, and poised to take on the world.

The younger, unmated females in Shiftertown were already giving Connor the eye, waiting for him to get through his Transition so they could pursue him as a potential mate. That would be interesting …

After a while, Carly sat up, pushing her hair from her face, and gently slid open the window of the cab. Tiger was still driving, alert but with his eyes closed. Empty desert was all around them now, the road straight.

"Hey," Carly said softly.

She still feared to startle him, but Tiger simply turned his head a little to listen to her.

"Think I could come back up there and drive?" Carly asked him. "This wind is playing hell with my hair. Besides, you look creepy."

Tiger opened his eyes all the way and frowned at her.

The pickup swerved onto the road's shoulder, and Connor groaned under the blanket. "We're goin' t'die. I know it."

Tiger growled. He slammed on the brakes, the truck vibrating on the rough pavement of the shoulder, but they came safely to a halt. The yellow grass beyond bent in the wind.

A few cars came up on them, none the SUV. The vehicles slid on by, not bothering them.

Carly climbed over the tailgate as quickly as her shaking legs would let her and ran to the driver's side door. Her sandals burned now from the roasting pavement beneath them.

"Coming, Con?" she asked over her shoulder.

Connor unzipped his hoodie but remained seated in the truck's bed. "Nah. Need another nap." He was a lion all right—they loved to sleep in the sun.

Carly leapt into the driver's seat and slammed the door, buckling up and checking the road behind her before she pulled out.

She glanced at Tiger, who'd moved to the passenger seat and now rested against the door.

"Do you have *any* idea where we're going?" she asked him as she sped up. "Besides *that way*?" She pointed forward.

"No," Tiger said. "I just know I have to go."

Carly let out a breath. "I can't say I understand, because I don't. But if it's what you need to do, then I'm with you."

Tiger studied her from golden eyes, his warmth a comfort after the glare of the sun. He said nothing for so long Carly wet her lips nervously.

"What?" she asked.

"I love you." The words were simple, spoken in Tiger's deep voice.

He didn't say it often. Carly knew he loved her—he showed her how much every day and every night. Had since the day they'd met.

But Tiger couldn't always get out the words that fit his feelings. Liam, in contrast, could be funny, wise, and caring, and find the right words for every occasion.

The Morrissey family's loquaciousness hadn't rubbed off on Tiger, who would remain mute while everyone else talked a mile a minute. Now Tiger's bald words filled the un-romantic pickup cab and entered Carly's heart.

"I love you too," she said softly.

If she hadn't had to drive, she'd have moved into his lap and thanked him with a deep kiss. As it was, Carly reached over and clasped his hand.

They shared a moment—understanding and love that didn't need words and flowery phrases. Tiger and Carly knew what was between them, the mate bond that wrapped around their hearts. That bond let them touch without touching, be a part of each other.

Carly squeezed Tiger's hand. When they were back home and out of danger, she'd show her love for him with something far beyond a little hand holding.

Tiger let out a grunt, and the returning pressure on her fingers grew suddenly tight. Tiger's face lost color as his eyes filled with pain, sweat beading on his skin.

"Not much time," he said thickly.

"Crap." Carly pressed the gas pedal. "Hang on, big guy."

Connor pulled his way up to the window. "They're coming."

Carly shot a look to the rearview mirror to see that, sure enough, a black SUV was gaining on them.

"Double crap." She slammed the pedal to the floor. "Guess there's no rest for the weary."

The pickup leapt forward, groaning and rattling, as they sped on into the flat New Mexico desert.

AT THE BORDER BETWEEN NEW MEXICO AND
Arizona, Tiger sensed a patrol car hiding in the
underpass of a little road that led to a tiny farm
town. He touched Carly's shoulder, and pointed.
"Cop."

"Shit." Carly took her foot off the accelerator and braked until they were going an even
75. Tiger kept his hand on her shoulder, liking
the warmth of her under his fingers.

"Well," Carly said brightly. "At least our
pursuers will have to slow down too or get
pulled over."

"The cops might be in on it with them,"
Tiger said. He didn't *know*, and this bothered
him. But the heart-wrenching cry in his head
wasn't letting him think straight.

Carly's eyes widened. "You think they
might be in cahoots?" she asked worriedly.
"Shit!"

She clenched the wheel and dragged in a
long breath as she passed the cop, doing exactly
the speed limit.

The Arizona DPS car's lights went on, and
sirens blared as the cop pulled out behind them
in a swirl of dust, following in fast pursuit. The

SUV hung back, letting the cop car get between them and the pickup.

Carly looked at Tiger, her beautiful eyes trusting. "What do you want me to do?"

There was no choice. "Go. Fast. I have to."

"You know, my sister wanted me to marry a man with a great job, a big house, and tons of cash," Carly said as she sped the pickup to eighty, eighty-five, ninety. "To think, right now I could be sitting by the pool buffing my nails and sipping a fancy cocktail."

She laughed, bubbling with mirth at a joke Tiger didn't really understand. He'd met the guy her sister had wanted Carly to marry—a weak, mean, irritating man who had already made her unhappy by the time Tiger came along. Why Carly thought that was funny, Tiger didn't know.

He only knew he liked hearing her laugh, that it eased the pain that sliced him, the urgency that drew him onward.

On rescue missions, he could feel the fear of the person he searched for, could sense their despair that no one would come. But usually it was distant, at the back of his mind, like a homing beacon to their location.

This person's distress gouged him, keeping

Tiger from feeling anything but the need to race to them.

If the DPS cop *wasn't* with the SUV guys, he or she could help. The SUV men might be hunting whoever Tiger sought, but a decent cop would bring backup, ambulances, humans trained to take care of others.

Humans like that did exist, in spite of the belief of some Shifters that all humans were barbaric to one another. Tiger had seen too many human men and women throwing themselves into danger on behalf of others to believe otherwise.

Carly passed a sign that announced they were in a town called Bowie. At the same time, Tiger's insides compressed with a sudden sharp pain. He doubled over, groaning.

"Tiger?" Carly's voice sounded far away. "You all right? Stay with me—Tiger?"

Tiger lifted a hand and waved at jagged mountains south of them. "There."

Carly peered at the mountains then scanned the road, including the two-exit town they were screaming through. Farms spread on either side of the freeway, the rich furrowed earth stretching out until it died into dust and desert.

The DPS car was still with them. As they left

Bowie, another raced down an onramp and joined in.

"How the hell am I going to get *there*?" Carly demanded. "This truck isn't exactly off-road material."

Tiger didn't know, and he couldn't think anymore. His head pounded, and he collapsed into the seat.

He heard Carly shout for Connor. When the lad finally rose to look in the window, Carly shoved her phone at him. "Bring up some maps. I need to know how to get over there." She pointed at the mountains.

Connor blinked, took in the cops chasing them, and then bent to the phone. His thumbs flew over it, Connor having taken to technology with startling ease. Though Shifters were restricted from having the latest gadgets, Connor knew all about them and how to manipulate them.

"There's a turnoff in Wilcox," Connor said over the wind. "Road heads toward those mountains. There's a national monument there."

He gave more directions to Carly, but Tiger couldn't make out his words.

He lapsed into darkness as Carly sped down the road, then she swerved off the freeway onto a highway that headed toward the looming crags.

We're coming, Tiger promised silently, but whether the person on the other end could hear him, he couldn't know.

CHAPTER FIVE

The road across the desert was narrow, a reddish-black ribbon unfolding through brush and dust. The vegetation was thicker here than in Texas and New Mexico, but spikier, as though the ground allowed only the hardiest plants to break through.

Carly straddled the yellow line on the empty road, going too fast to worry about the rules. Behind her came four DPS officers, weaving in and out and around the black SUV. Connor had sunk lower into the truck bed, holding on as Carly careened down the road.

More worrying to Carly was Tiger. Sweat dampened his hair and growls issued from his throat.

She recognized the signs—he wanted to shift to let the tiger in him take over. But a giant Bengal filling the cab of the small truck right now would be a disaster.

"Hang on," Carly said to him.

Tiger didn't answer. Carly couldn't reach over and reassure him with a touch, because she didn't dare let go of the wheel.

A sign told her she was heading toward Chiricahua National Monument. That meant a gatehouse at the end of the road—probably—where a park ranger would be there to provide helpful information.

If Carly stopped, the cops would be all over them, and the cops were armed. If Tiger jumped out and ran, the police would have no hesitation about shooting.

Tiger had the tendency to shake off bullets though—Carly had witnessed this. On the other hand, enough bullets would bring even Tiger down. Out in the middle of nowhere, with no hospital or Shifter healer in sight, Tiger would die.

Carly didn't slow. Unlike Hill Country in Texas, there were no side roads here, nothing but an empty plain covered with rocks and scrub, and mountains that looked more craggy the closer she drew to them.

Trees began to dot the desert, small, low-crowned mesquite at first. As the land rose, the trees became hardwoods and pines, dried grasses beneath them.

The road started to wind, the pavement narrowing, but Carly didn't slow.

She saw the gatehouse ahead. Her heart pounded and her throat closed up. The road became a single lane with signs telling her to proceed at a crawl.

The truck left the pavement as Carly swerved around the gatehouse. She understood then why Dylan drove a slim, maneuverable pickup. Instead of bottoming out or skidding on the soft dirt, the truck gripped the earth and flew past the gatehouse.

The guard inside stepped out then hurriedly pulled himself back in as they zoomed past. Carly lifted one hand in apology.

She raced along the empty, winding road, sparing an occasional glance into the rearview mirror. The wide SUV and DPS cars had to slow at the narrow entrance and sort themselves out, giving Carly a few seconds' advantage.

Connor pulled himself up and looked back. Carly couldn't hear what he yelled, but he pounded the air in triumph. So much for not taunting their pursuers.

The road climbed, the curves becoming sinuous. Carly desperately cranked the wheel to keep from going over the edge of the precipitous road while they went up and up.

"Stop!" Tiger's shout tore through the wind and roar of the engine.

Carly jammed her feet onto the brake pedal, sending the truck sliding toward the cliff's edge, spinning the steering wheel to bring them to safer ground.

Tiger leapt out, his door slamming before Carly came to a complete halt. Without looking back, Tiger sprinted into the thick woods, his clothes falling into shreds as he shifted.

Carly watched him disappear under the trees, and then she was surrounded by flashing lights, cars, and men in uniform drawing weapons. The men in black fatigues piled out of the SUV and rushed after Tiger.

"Hands on the wheel, ma'am," one of the DPS officers told her.

His pistol pointed right at Carly's head. She clung to the steering wheel, not moving an inch.

She was going to be arrested and hauled off for running from the cops and for helping

Shifters break all kinds of laws. And she didn't care. What happened to her didn't matter, as long as Tiger got away.

Another officer reached into the truck's bed and pulled aside the blankets.

He shouted and backpedalled as a lion, his black mane not fully grown, leapt from the bed at him, his jaws open, all his teeth bared.

TIGER, NOW A TIGER, PAUSED AND LOOK BACK as he crested the hill.

The pickup was surrounded by police, cops training their pistols on Carly. She sat still, her fear coming through the mate bond to him. He felt her determination as well, yelling at him to go on. *I'll be fine.*

He saw Connor leap from the truck's bed, his sparking Collar trying to stop him. The cops leapt back in stunned surprise, but they recovered quickly and brought their weapons to bear.

Connor bounded over the heads of the cops and charged off into the woods. *Distracting them from Carly,* the logical part of Tiger's brain told him. *Protecting her.*

Even so, Tiger headed down toward the

truck again. As much danger as the one awaiting rescue was in, his mate and Connor needed his immediate help.

He moved through the trees in a silent streak, with the incredible stealth of his Bengal. He'd take out the remaining police, get Carly to safety, and then continue his mission.

The men from the SUV who'd started up the hill drew near, and Tiger halted, crouching under the striped shadows of a stand of trees. They passed him without noticing, flowing on up the hill.

The men weren't looking for him, Tiger realized after a moment. They weren't searching —they were making for a specific destination. Tiger knew without doubt they were heading for the one he was here to rescue.

Pain lashed at him. Tiger stifled his huff of breath, remaining utterly still. Instead of fading, the pain blossomed and surged, wrapping around his brain and stifling any rational thought.

Tiger had to protect his mate. She was the most important thing in his world. If he lost Carly, he would die of the grief.

But he'd never felt the need to find someone as sharply as he did now. The numbers behind his eyelids sped into a blur, and agony laced his every nerve.

Help me, came the faint cry.

Not in words. The call was visceral, enveloping Tiger in a grip he could not shake.

He saw Carly talking through the window to the police, her hands on the steering wheel. She was shaking her head at them, her eyes wide as she emphasized her words.

Carly could talk. And flash that beautiful smile. And have everyone in the world eating out of her hand.

The cops wouldn't hurt her—at least, they weren't supposed to. She was human, not threatening them. Connor was the threat, and he currently was running faster than fast up the slopes of the mountain, two officers and a park ranger chasing him, struggling to catch him.

Tiger couldn't see Connor at the moment, but he sensed him as he sensed everything in these mountains—the nervous animals wondering at the new predators in their midst, the adrenaline rush and fear of the men chasing Connor, as well as hikers about ten miles away, unaware of any drama.

Another whiplash of torment had Tiger on

his feet. He sent a surge of love to Carly and turned to run up the hill.

These mountains were a vast network of little valleys and streams. Hills covered with trees and scrub wound around vertical columns of rocks that appeared to be a series of boulders balanced on top of each other. *Hoodoos*—the vast store of knowledge in Tiger's brain dredged up the word.

Tiger noted the landscape in passing while he kept running, following both his instincts and the men in black. He moved around a thicket of the standing rocks and plunged into shadows between them.

He came out the other side and halted in surprise.

In front of him was a small frame house on a flat piece of land, in a clearing surrounded by thick junipers and the twisted forms of pinyon pine. The air was much cooler at this elevation, exactly thirty-five degrees cooler, Tiger knew, in Fahrenheit. Nineteen point four degrees cooler in centigrade.

The distress signal came from the house.

Tiger crouched under a particularly gnarled pine, its scent sharp.

He heard nothing. No screams for help, not

even the whimpering of a child or the despondent thoughts of an adult fearing they'd never be found.

No scent either, except the plants and trees that grew in profusion around the clearing. Strange. There should be *something*. Tiger had a better sense of smell than any Shifter he knew. How was it that he scented nothing from the house?

As he watched, the men from the SUV came into the clearing from another trail. They were panting, weapons shouldered, tired from the climb.

There were four of them, human men with hair from blond to the deep black of the black-skinned man. Though the climb had winded them, they glanced around with alertness, trained soldiers wary of their surroundings.

They weren't Shifter Bureau. While they wore black fatigues similar to the ones of the men attached to Shifter Bureau, they weren't quite the same, and the uniforms had no insignia.

Freelance, Tiger reasoned. Mercenaries. But working for whom?

These thoughts went through the back of

Tiger's mind as anguish blotted out all else. *I don't know what to do. It hurts. Help me!*

One of the men—dark brown hair, dark skin, brown eyes, lined face—gave the signal to approach the house. They never noticed Tiger lying in the shadows, didn't even look for him.

The leader walked to the house, swiped a key card into a lock, and disappeared inside. The other three, with another glance around the clearing, followed.

In the brief space the door was open, Tiger at last caught scent. He smelled stark fear, confusion, rage, confinement, frustration. And most of all—Shifter. A very specific Shifter. *Son of a bitch.*

As the door swung shut, Tiger ran on noiseless feet to the house, but he wasn't in time to catch the door.

The keycard reader, a faceless metal slot on a rather ordinary door, seemed to mock him. Tiger put a paw on the slot, but there was nothing but smooth metal under his claws. No convenient keypad so he could crack the code, no lock to pick.

He snarled. Inside was a Shifter in peril, and those determined men were now inside with it.

Tiger rose on his hind legs, shifting to the

beast that was halfway between a tiger and man. This shape was powerful though exhausting, but in it he could use his human hands with the strength of his tiger.

He dug his fingers into the doorframe, and ripped the door and frame from the wall.

Tiger tossed the pieces aside, his hands streaming blood, and ducked through the opening. He remained his half beast and kept to the shadows, knowing the noise he'd made had announced his presence.

Tiger snarled, letting the low, guttural sound of the Bengal fill up the empty spaces, and he strode forward to see what fate awaited him.

CHAPTER SIX

A re y'all gonna help me, or not?" Carly demanded.

She suppressed a shiver as the two cops frowned, looking pretty sure that Carly was a harmless woman from Texas drawn in to this adventure by accident. But they were still mistrustful.

One of the policemen was named Kirk, the other Tyson, or Ty for short. Carly had learned that much about them.

They knew all about *her*, because they'd taken her driver's license and checked her out on their computer. They knew Carly's middle name, her birthdate, her address, her license number, and that she'd had the photo taken right after a dusty drive back from New Orleans where she'd been visiting cousins and so her hair had been a mess. She'd volunteered that last part.

No, the truck wasn't hers, Carly confessed. She'd borrowed it from her next-door neighbor, which was true.

She had no idea if Dylan would vouch for her, but he'd never let Tiger's mate be led off to jail, right? Tiger would strenuously object—he wasn't afraid of Dylan, one of the few Shifters who wasn't. Dylan had to know that.

"I'm really worried about Connor," Carly told Kirk and Ty now. "He's just a youngster. Please don't let anyone hurt him. He won't attack if he's not provoked." Carly mentally crossed her fingers as she said this. She had no idea what Connor might do in his rampage.

Kirk had already been on his radio telling the other two state cops who'd followed to not shoot the lion—he was a pet. He'd also alerted more park rangers, who were on their way with tranq rifles. They dealt with wild animals all the time.

"Keeping exotic animals isn't exactly legal, ma'am," Ty said in a kind but firm voice. The two officers hadn't stumbled onto the fact that

Connor was a Shifter—they thought him a real lion. In fact, they weren't sure why they'd been recruited to help the men in the black SUV. They'd gotten orders to assist, and they'd assisted.

Carly opened her eyes wide. "Connor isn't exotic. He's one of the family." Which was true.

Damn it, Tiger, where are you and are you all right?

Kirk's radio clicked. Carly heard the voice come through—*He's heading for the old ranch house at the end of Vista Trail. We're in pursuit.*

She knew Connor had run off to distract the cops from Tiger and Carly, to divide and weaken their forces. But Connor would now have to evade capture himself.

"Y'all are saying there's a ranch out here?" Carly asked in her best this-little-ole-Texas-girl-needs-the-men-to-explain-everything-to-her voice.

"Up at the top of this hill," Ty pointed the direction Tiger had run.

All Carly could see were trees, rocks, and blue sky. It was gorgeous out here; the view down the slope showed pillars of rocks and peaks of mountains seemingly without end. Maybe she and Tiger could come back here one day and visit like tourists.

She breathed out. Making plans, even tenuous ones, helped her believe they'd all get out of this and safely home.

"Does the road go up there?" Carly shaded her eyes against the afternoon sun and peered worriedly through the trees.

"Yes, but you're staying right here, ma'am," Tyson answered. He was the friendlier of the two, and smiled now, so that his eyes crinkled.

"But I might be able to calm Connor down. He's used to me. He'll panic if he sees all those rangers and policemen. It will be less dangerous to y'all if I'm there."

Kirk shook his head. "Not taking a civilian into a risky situation."

Carly let her lip tremble, not hard to do in her agitated state. "We love Connor. If anything happens to him, I'll just die. He's a sweetheart most of the time. Likes to eat burgers and watch TV with us." Again, every word the truth.

Tyson looked sympathetic. Maybe he liked animals too. "If she can help catch him ..." he said to his colleague.

"Bad idea," Kirk snapped. Carly was definitely not liking him.

Tyson considered. "If it makes a difference between this lion attacking and us getting a clean shot with a tranq rifle, I'm gonna risk it. You ride with me, Ms. Randal."

"Sure thing." Carly grabbed her purse and hurried after Tyson as he walked to his patrol car.

She hopped into the front seat of Tyson's DPS car while he slid into the driver's side. "We'll have to take the lion to animal control," Tyson said, apologetic. "But don't worry too much. If he's healthy and tame, there are places around who adopt big cats. They'll probably let you visit him."

What a nice guy, Carly thought with a pang as she tried to look sorrowful. She felt guilty for deceiving him, but not guilty enough to put Connor and Tiger in danger.

Tyson smoothly pulled out, his engine humming as steadily Dylan's truck's. This car, though, didn't rattle and groan as Tyson did a one-eighty in the dirt and drove back onto the narrow road.

The pavement climbed, a cliff dropping away to the right, heart-stoppingly close to Carly's door. She could look all the way down to a river glittering at the bottom of a canyon.

If Connor chose to lose himself here, he'd be difficult to find, Tiger even harder.

"Beautiful isn't it?" Tyson asked her cheerfully. "It's a great place for camping and hiking. Birding too, if you like that."

Poor Tyson. He'd be asking her on a camping date before long. Carly might be amused at his interest if she weren't so worried about Tiger and Connor.

"Yeah, it's pretty." Carly tried to sound offhand while she anxiously scanned the woods for any sign of Shifters.

Tyson turned the car onto a narrower road that led through trees, leaving the cliffs behind. After about a mile, he pulled into a wider dirt space and shut off the engine.

"Ranch house is just up this path. You might want to stay here." Tyson opened the door and hopped out, carefully taking the keys with him.

No way Carly was sitting here while armed men went after her mate and Connor. She pulled herself out of the car as soon as Tyson disappeared beneath the trees and hurried quietly after him, holding her purse against her side so it wouldn't flap around.

The path was overgrown but discernible. She glimpsed Tyson ahead of her, his dark blue uniform flashing between green pine needles and the white-gray twists of bare branches.

Not far up the hill the trees parted to reveal a small clearing with a house in the middle of it. It had obviously been painted and kept up at one time, but now the paint was peeling, the weather wearing down the wooden house and the gingerbread on the porch. The front garden was a crop of weeds with a few cultivated flowers struggling through.

Carly noted all this distractedly, because what mostly stood out about the house was the front door. It had been ripped from the wall and now lay in the weeds, wildflowers straggling around it.

From the opening of the discarded door, Carly heard roaring, which didn't quite drown out the men screaming. Tyson slowed, drew his gun, and approached.

Carly put on a burst of speed and ran past him, up the steps, across the creaking porch floor, and right into the house. Tyson shouted at her, but Carly didn't stop.

"Tiger?"

She heard her mate's unmistakable growls, the deep, rumbling breathy snarls of an enraged tiger.

The entire place wasn't that big—it reminded her of the farmhouse in the old

Wizard of Oz movie. Carly looked into the three downstairs rooms and found them empty, dusty, and forlorn.

The staircase leading to the second floor didn't look stable, but the noises weren't coming from up there. They came from the open door under the staircase, from which a set of cement steps led downward.

Carly didn't hesitate. Down she went.

The basement was a hell of a lot bigger than the upstairs. The walls that ran back into the hill were lined with stone, the ceiling shored up with thick timber beams. It made Carly think of the secret places Shifters built under their houses to store the wealth or treasured objects they'd accumulated over their lengthy lives. They made these spaces into their hideaways, where they could be themselves, with their families, away from human eyes.

The staircase emptied into a large, blank room lit by one overhead fluorescent light. Across this room was an opening that led to another chamber, the door that had closed it now torn from its hinges and lying discarded to one side. Tiger had definitely been here.

Tyson arrived at the bottom of the stairs, breathless, his pistol drawn.

"You need to stay behind me," he snapped at Carly.

Not while Tiger was in trouble she didn't. Carly trotted forward, peering into the next room to find it led to yet another one, with *its* door also on the floor.

Carly went inside and to the next chamber, also empty, also lit by one light. She moved cautiously, but quickly, the need to reach Tiger acute.

"Carly," Tyson tried again.

First names already, is it? Carly thought without slowing.

Tyson let out a startled cry, and Carly heard more growling behind her. She turned in time to see a lion charge past Tyson then brush by her, heading into the bowels of the basement.

"Connor!" He was running to rescue Tiger, the big sweetheart. Except that was a sure way to get himself killed.

Carly hurried after him, following Connor through room after room. Every single one had once had a thick door with an electronic lock closing it off. Every single door was now a mangled wreck beside the opening it had sealed.

The rooms at last ended in one that must be a hundred feet long. By the flicker of a fluorescent light, Carly saw thick iron bars enclosing the far end of the room, with a solid wall behind that. No more doors.

Tiger stood in the middle of this room, fearsome in his half-man, half-tiger form, facing down at least a dozen men. Carly recognized the black fatigues of the guys from the SUV. They'd been joined by others, though she'd seen no one else come up the road. That meant the other soldiers had already been here.

Connor joined Tiger, who snarled warningly at the men surrounding them. One soldier brought up a tranq rifle and shot at Connor, but Connor wasn't where he'd been a second before. He sprang from all four paws straight into the air, twisting himself around to land in front of another startled soldier.

The tranq dart flew past Connor and at Carly. She didn't have time to duck, but the trajectory let the dart sail past her with an inch to spare, before it embedded itself in Tyson's shoulder.

Tranqs for Shifters were strong. Tyson took one step before his legs folded up, his eyes rolled back in his head, and he went down.

His radio crackled, a voice demanding to know where Tyson was and what was going on.

Carly ignored it but picked up Tyson's pistol from his slack hand and tucked it safely back into its holster.

The man with the tranq rifle tried frantically to reload. Tiger knocked the gun out of his hands and the man to the floor after it.

Another of the soldiers raised a tranq rifle, a look of triumph on his face as he shot a dart straight into Tiger's stomach.

Tiger grabbed the dart, yanked it from his furred flesh, and tossed it aside. The shooter's eyes widened just before Tiger grabbed the rifle from his hands and broke it in half.

Tranqs didn't always work on Tiger. He had to be shot multiple times before they even slowed him down. Connor called him a Super Shifter, and told Tiger he should wear a cape. Tiger never answered this, but last Halloween, he'd taken some cubs trick-or-treating through Shiftertown with a red blanket hanging down his back.

The laid-back, cub-loving Tiger was absent here. He had these guys terrified, but they were holding him at bay, keeping Tiger from reaching the cage at the end of the room.

Why?

Carly, unnoticed by everyone except Tiger,

slipped around them all and made for the far wall.

The first thing Carly noted as she neared the cage was the smell. The stench of waste and unwashed being hit her with a slap.

The second thing was the sound. Tiger's snarling and now Connor's had covered the growls of the other animal in the room.

Those growls escalated to a near shriek as Carly drew near. The cage was in deep shadow, and Carly crept closer, wishing for a flashlight.

Something moved beyond the bars, a being that paced restlessly, a wild thing trapped. Occasionally that thing leapt against the cage. The bars rattled under the assault but held.

Back to pacing, the sound coming from the beast's mouth frantic and enraged. Carly had become more attuned to wild animals after living for a year with Shifters, and she understood that beneath this creature's rage and frustration was terrible fear and pain.

This was what Tiger must have sensed, the beast's call for help that reached across eight hundred miles of desert.

"It's all right," Carly soothed as she took the last steps to the cage. "Tiger's here to help you."

The creature chose that moment to slam itself into the bars, inches from Carly.

In the dim light, Carly saw a body of thick fur, long, razor-sharp claws, and a red mouth with huge, gleaming teeth.

But that was not what made Carly step back in shock. What made her gasp was the fact that the fur was striped, and the eyes that glared at her with such ferocity were a wild, golden yellow.

Tiger eyes.

CHAPTER SEVEN

Tiger knew when Carly made a connection with the other tiger. The constant wail of fear dimmed as surprise sparked through it.

The men fighting Tiger did *not* want Tiger or Connor at the cage. They were stubborn, desperate—one yelled into a radio that they needed more backup.

That backup would arrive soon, and they might have enough tranqs or bullets between them to knock out Tiger. Then they'd take Connor and Carly, and the tiger he'd come to rescue wouldn't stand a chance.

But no way in hell would he give up. He wasn't leaving the tiger behind, not if he had to crush every man in his way.

"Tiger!" he heard Carly call.

Tiger didn't dare take time to respond, continuing to feint against the men who surrounded him. He didn't want to kill any of them, but he would if they left him no choice.

He still didn't know exactly who they were, but he knew *what* they were. Guards charged with keeping the beast in the cage from ever leaving, with keeping Tiger away from it. Whether they understood why or were just following orders, Tiger couldn't tell, and it didn't matter. They were the enemy at the moment, and he had to get past them.

Connor fought and ducked with the agility of a young cat, twisting and turning, never taking a hit. A soldier aimed at him with another tranq rifle.

Once again, Connor leapt to be elsewhere when the tranq gun went off. The dart bounced harmlessly off the floor, its barb breaking.

Connor came down into a low crouch. When he sprang again, he sailed over the heads of their attackers and landed by Carly and the cage.

The tiger inside roared in fury. It slammed against the bars, huge claws trying to thrust through. The bars were too narrow for that, and the tiger's paws stuck. It yanked them free, more enraged and terrified than ever.

Peace, little one, Tiger tried to tell it through whatever link they'd formed. He didn't speak in words but with the sense of them. *He's a friend.*

He felt the tiger latch onto the last word, puzzling over it. *Friend.* It didn't understand the concept.

Which was why Tiger was taking the beast out of there and home with them. He'd fight every man in this room and whatever truckloads of backup troops they threw at him to make sure it happened. He'd fight to his dying breath.

Through the mate bond, he knew that Carly understood. Tiger's heart flooded with love for her. She *knew.* They had a connection like no other.

There was a reason Tiger had known Carly was his mate from the first moment he'd seen her. The other Shifters had told him he was mistaken—Shifter mating didn't work like that —but Tiger hadn't listened to them. And he'd been right.

Thank you, Tiger whispered through the bond, and felt Carly's love in response.

THE TIGER THREW ITSELF AT THE BARS AGAIN.
Carly backed a step, but Connor had gone
completely still, his lion eyes wide.

Then Connor's limbs began to crackle,
sinews stretching and twisting as he rose into his
human form. His black mane shrank down to
become human hair, and his nose receded to
make his blue eyes prominent.

A few seconds later, he was on his human
feet, without a shred of clothing, his muscles
as hard as his uncles'. He'd grown into his
man's body in the last year, his lankiness nearly
gone.

"Holy fucking shit." His words were soft,
Connor caught in astonishment.

The tiger, who'd stilled while Connor had
shifted, switched its full focus on him, no more
snarling or striking.

Now Carly heard *its* bones and sinews crack-
ling as Connor's had, even over Tiger's roaring
and the soldier's shouts.

The tiger shrank down into a lithe human
body, as honed as all Shifters were. The fur
became black and orange hair, like Tiger's, only
this hair was long and filthy, a tangled mass.
They'd need a ton of shampoo and conditioner
to save it.

"Holy fucking shit!" Connor's statement was loud this time.

"Exactly," Carly whispered, her throat closing.

The Shifter in front of them was female. She stood almost as tall as Connor, who had the Morrissey height, but she wasn't a youngster. Her breasts and hips were full, and her face, which was stark with fear, held the softness of a young woman, one around Carly's age, maybe a little younger. Shifters aged differently from humans, and Shifters in their twenties were still considered cubs. This girl could be on either side of the line.

Carly would call her beautiful if not for the cuts and bruises all over her body. She realized that the pattern of bruises on her thighs and sides came from the cage's bars, the cuts, from her own claws.

The poor thing was crazed with terror and frustration, anger and despair. She'd only ceased rampaging for the moment because of her astonishment at Connor.

Connor managed to close his gaping mouth. "It's all right," he told the tiger-girl cheerfully through the bars. "We're here to rescue you."

The tiger-girl gave him another look of

confusion, right before a wave of madness twisted her face. She doubled over as though cramps wracked her body, and she clutched at her hair, tearing out a hunk. Her fists balled and she struck the floor, screaming in agony.

Carly's heart twisted. She wanted to help the creature but had no idea how. The cage had no lock or door she could see—the bars were drilled directly into the walls and ceiling. They probably shoved food through those bars to her, too afraid to go inside. Bastards.

They would take her out of there. They had to. Not only was this woman a Shifter, but Carly put together the stories Tiger had told her about himself and his past, the time factor, and Tiger's strange and desperate need to reach this place.

Carly understood everything. She wanted to break down and cry, but that wouldn't do any good, would it?

Tiger must know that this was more than a simple search and rescue. Carly wondered if the soldiers trying so hard to stop him knew too. They were like the men Tiger had told her about who'd guarded him in Area 51, soldiers charged with helping the researchers keep him confined and subdued.

Meanwhile, the tiger-girl was bellowing her

anguish. She shifted into her half-beast, her screams turning to nonstop snarls. She was fearsome—towering over both Carly and Connor, her claws long and curved.

"Hey!" Connor shouted at her. "It's all right. If you don't fight it, it won't be so bad, at least that's what Scott told me." He let out a breath and turned to Carly. "Shit, do you think she can understand me?"

"I don't know," Carly said shakily. "Depends on how long she's been locked in there. And if people bother to talk to her."

Connor put his hand around the bars. The tiger-beast swung to him, her yellow eyes fixed on his face. Carly held her breath, waiting for an attack, but the tiger-girl only stared at Connor.

"Tran-si-tion," Connor spoke the word slowly and carefully. "That's what's going on with you, lass. All Shifters go through it when they're coming of age. I guess it's your time."

The tiger-girl breathed heavily, growls in her throat. But she'd quieted, cocking her head at Connor's voice.

"There you go," Connor said. "It's hell, I'm told. I can't *wait* to experience it, right? I have a few more years to go, if I'm lucky. Though Uncle Sean tells me the males of my family reach it faster than most. My dad went through it when he was only a year older than I am. Just great, I said."

The tiger-girl shifted back down to human with a rapidity Carly had only ever seen Tiger achieve. Most Shifters struggled a bit, and the ability varied from Shifter to Shifter.

The tiger-girl continued to stare at Connor, her sides rising and falling with her sharp breaths.

"Can you understand us?" Carly asked her in a soft voice.

The tiger-girl jerked her head to look at Carly without comprehension then moved back to Connor.

"It's all right," Connor said to her. "Like I say, we've come to rescue you."

The noise of more soldiers rushing in to join the fight put paid to that claim. Men in black fatigues poured through the door, all carrying firearms, of which some were tranq rifles. Kirk and several other DPS officers plus the park rangers came behind them, Kirk rushing to Tyson to pull his inert body out of the way.

Carly's heart sped with fear. Even Tiger was no match for thirty men with weapons. She imagined him going down, bloody and fighting for his last breath.

No. Carly thought of baby Seth waiting for them back in Austin, his silky hair with the orange and black stripes of his father. She glanced at the tiger-girl, savage with isolation and fear, trapped behind permanent bars, a prisoner for who knew how many years.

No!

Carly ran toward the men who flowed around her mate, pushing herself between them and Tiger. She held out her hands.

"Y'all have to *stop!*"

A few of the men did halt, if only in shock that a small woman with messy hair and a Texas accent had darted in to scold them.

"Come on now," Carly went on, trying to get the words out before she lost her nerve. "You have a helpless young woman in a *cage*, for crying out loud. I know she's Shifter, but she should go to a Shiftertown. With us. We'll take care of her now."

Brave words. No one lowered a weapon. Tiger had paused, but his growls didn't cease. Carly knew that as soon as she was safely out of the way, he'd attack again. His protective instinct wouldn't let him stop.

One man lowered his weapon and moved toward her. "Orders, ma'am. *We* contain the Shifter. No one takes it."

"Her," Carly said angrily. "She's a *her*, not an *it*. And I wouldn't touch me, if I were you."

The man ignored the warning and reached for her. "You need to go. If I have to carry you out I will."

Carly took a step back from his outstretched fingers and stumbled into Tiger. "I'm his *mate*. If you touch me, he'll kill you, and I don't think I can stop him."

Tiger steadied Carly and an instant later was between her and the soldier. That man's eyes widened in alarm just before Tiger's fist caught him on the side of the head. He went down in an ungainly heap of black fatigues.

The other men took that as a signal to attack. Carly screamed and ducked as guns went off.

Over at the cage, Connor had changed to his lion-beast. He was pulling at the bars, encouraging the tiger-girl to join in trying to break them. Carly saw the tiger-girl putting her hands above Connor's, both of them tugging, but to no avail.

At the same time three tranq darts and a couple of bullets went straight into Tiger.

Tiger went very still. At a shouted command, the men ceased fire.

Tiger turned his half-beast's head to study each of the men in turn, pinning them with his golden gaze even as blood flowed down his furred torso. The men froze, staring at him in a daze. Though they'd likely been trained to fight Shifters, Carly could guarantee they'd never seen anything like Tiger before.

Tiger watched them watch him, the rumbles in his throat not diminishing.

It usually took five or so doses of tranquilizer meant for a normal Shifter to bring down Tiger, and then only if he was tired. He'd shrug off a bullet or two as well. The researchers who'd made him had designed him to survive long after any other Shifter would have died.

Carly slowly stood up, reaching to slide her hand over Tiger's clenched, clawed one. The touch of mate healed, he'd told her, and Carly would hold him together with all her might.

"Captain—Sergeant—whoever you are," Carly said rapidly to the one who'd given the command to cease firing. "If Tiger decides to, he can kill everyone in this room without sweating very much. He doesn't want to, which is why y'all are still alive. Can't you see how cruel it is to keep that poor woman in a cage? Let us take her away with us."

The man she addressed had the hard-eyed expression of one who wasn't going to be easily swayed. "She's a dangerous animal, ma'am. Not like a Shifter. Our orders are to keep her here, and we're keeping her here."

"Who do you work for? Shifter Bureau? Or the army? Or the Fae?"

He watched her with an impenetrable gaze.

"What if you had different orders?" Carly persisted. "What if you had orders to let her go?"

The man's eyes narrowed. "But I don't, do I? I respect the chain of command. And this really isn't your business, ma'am."

"She's a Shifter, so yes, it is my business. Now, I'm going to make a phone call. All right?" Carly pulled her phone from the purse she was still madly clutching. The phone thankfully had a charge, though the readout showed she wasn't getting any reception.

"Okay, so I'll have to go outside to make the call." Damn it—why did the brilliant technology of the twenty-first century fail when it was needed most? "Just put the blood bath on hold, all right? Shifter Bureau's going to want to know about this."

Shifter Bureau was far more interested in containing Shifters and subduing them than helping them, it was true. But one man, the liaison between the Austin Shiftertown and its local Shifter Bureau, could help. Walker Danielson was mated to a Shifter—a Kodiak bear—and he understood Shifters better than any human in the Bureau ever could.

If she could get Walker involved, he could talk to the Shifter Bureau for this state and have the tiger-girl transferred to the Austin Shiftertown. This would take an unbelievable amount of time, but if Walker put things in motion, at least these fanatic men might stop trying to kill Tiger.

The man in charge flicked his fingers. "Take her out."

Not to make a phone call, Carly was thinking. Three men detached themselves from the group and came at her.

Tiger spun, yanked the pistols from two of the advancing men's grips, and crushed them between his fingers. As the pieces of metal rained to the floor, every gun barrel trained on him.

"No!" Carly screamed. She flung herself in front of her mate, just as the noise of gunfire filled the room.

CHAPTER EIGHT

F or Tiger, everything suddenly became very clear.

He saw Carly with her arms outstretched, pasting herself against the front of his bloody body. He heard Connor shouting and saw the men's fingers move on triggers.

The tiger-girl's wail cut through the noise and fired Tiger's blood like a burning electric wire.

Save her …

There was no other option.

Tiger lifted Carly from her feet an instant before the weapons went off. She made the "Eep!" sound she liked to when he did something unexpected, and then she was out of the way.

Tiger kept turning after he let her go, kicking to sweep those closing in on him off their feet. He moved so fast that by the time the guns went off he'd destroyed their aim. Men ducked, cursed, and pointed pistols up or downward to keep bullets from hitting their fellows.

Once they regained their bearings, they'd shoot again, thirty men determined to take Tiger down.

Didn't matter. Tiger trusted that Carly and Connor would get the tiger-girl to safety while he finished this.

He launched into his enemies, not holding back. He barely felt the bullets embed in his body, another dose of tranq entering his blood.

Carly's touch had helped ease his initial pain and erase the drugs trying to seep through him. He was stronger for it, able to resist the barrage that came at him now.

Tiger's most basic instinct was not to kill. He'd been made to help, not hurt.

But sometimes …

Carly yelled. Connor echoed the cry, the word sounding like *Here!*

Now more men were in the room. They also

wore black, but the uniforms weren't the same. The commander of the new troop had very short white-blond hair, light blue eyes, and a hard face. Behind him came three Shifters, all black-haired and blue-eyed, and all very pissed off.

"Tiger!" Walker Danielson's voice sliced through his haze. "Stand down. We got this."

The man in charge of the enemy soldiers snapped, "Who the fuck are you?"

"Major Danielson, Sergeant. This is my op now."

Tiger wasn't sure how Walker knew the man was a sergeant, but the sergeant came to stiff if angry attention and popped off a salute.

"Yes, *sir*." The obedience was belligerent, but given.

"Tiger, lad …"

Liam Morrissey, followed by his father and his brother, the latter with the huge Sword of the Guardian sheathed on his back, waded through the hostile men.

Won't be needing the sword today, Tiger thought dimly.

All three Morrisseys headed for Tiger, but Tiger turned his back on them and strode for the cage, coming down out of his tiger-beast as he went.

Connor at the cage became human again, his face draining of color when he saw his uncles and grandfather. "Oh, shite."

Behind him, the young woman grabbed the bars, her cries escalating to shrieks as she tried to break them. Her distress beat on Tiger, the need to help her battering all else aside.

He reached the cage. Carly looked up at him in perfect understanding. The fact that she knew exactly what was going on without Tiger having to say a word made the ache of his injuries recede. She was the mate of his heart in the truest sense of the word.

Tiger seized the bars of the cage and pulled.

"Tried that," Connor said. "The two of us couldn't budge them. It's some kind of Shifter-resistant metal or something."

Tiger didn't answer. He let go, closed his eyes, put both hands on one bar, turned side-ways, and *pushed*.

The tiger-girl inside didn't wait. She seized the bar and pushed with him, her wordless cries filled with determination.

Behind him, Walker barked commands. "Get that cage open," was one of them.

"It's sealed," the sergeant said, sounding triumphant. "No one goes in or out."

Tiger sensed the sea of bodies parting for Dylan Morrissey. That happened for Dylan. The older Shifter, who'd seen everything and been through so much, said nothing as he walked to them, only took hold of the bar around Tiger's grip and leant his strength.

"Come on then, Sean," Liam said. "We can't let Dad show us up."

Two more pairs of hands joined in, and then Connor's. Liam's voice sounded again, directed at Connor. "I'll be talking to *you* later."

Connor moaned. "Oh, man, I am so screwed."

His chagrin agitated the tiger-girl, who snarled at Liam. Liam huffed a laugh. "Kill me later, sweetheart," he said. "Let's get you out of this first."

Carly came to help, grasping the bars below Tiger's grip. She couldn't make a dent, and he knew it, yet she refused to stand and do nothing. Another thing Tiger loved about her.

The iron bar creaked, bent, and then broke. A sound like a thunderclap rang through the room, and dust and pebbles rained down from the cement ceiling.

Tiger ripped the pieces of bar away, and then started on the next one.

With the Morrisseys and the tiger-girl helping, the second bar broke more rapidly, the desert-dried rock above crumbling into a white rain.

Tiger reached in and yanked the young woman out of the cage. She shrieked and fought, her terror renewed. She wanted out, but she didn't know who all these men were—men who had caged her, just as they'd caged Tiger once upon a time.

Tiger dragged the tiger-girl against him. She struggled and struck out, her blows on his wounded body hurting, but Tiger stood firm.

He put his hands around her face and tilted her head up so that she looked into his eyes. Tiger studied hers, yellow irises with flecks of deep gold, the eyes of a tiger.

The young woman at last stilled, staring at him in disbelief. Then she gave another cry, one of awakening, awareness, and hope.

She flung her arms around Tiger, and he gathered her to him. Her tangled and ruined hair was rough against his cheek, and she was shaking all over, but he held her hard, a grief he'd embraced for nearly thirty years loosening and flowing away.

He heard Liam's intake of breath. "Goddess, what the hell is he doing?"

And then came Carly's beautiful laugh. "He's doing what's only natural, Liam Morrissey. Don't you get it? She's his *cub*."

CHAPTER NINE

C arly melted close to Tiger as he held on to the cub that had been taken from him so many years ago.

He'd told Carly the tale—he'd been forced to breed, right after his Transition, with another Shifter woman who had then died bringing in the baby. They'd showed Tiger the cub briefly then taken it away, explaining to him later that it had died.

They'd also told him his cub had been a son. The baby had been wrapped up and they hadn't allowed him to touch it.

Tiger might not have been able to tell the difference at that point, or know enough how to. He'd barely been out of cubhood himself.

Why this girl had been brought here and caged Carly didn't know. More experiments probably. Shifters had been used for those even before they were outed.

"Hey, big guy." Liam Morrissey's voice was gentle, the purr of his cat coming through. "We need to go. Don't worry—she's coming with us."

The soldiers guarding the tiger-girl moved restlessly. They seemed inclined to obey Walker —the sergeant said he respected the chain of command. But, Carly sensed, only until the sergeant decided Walker didn't have authority in this situation. From the little Walker had told her about the military, officers and NCOs didn't always see eye to eye.

"Take her out, Tiger," Walker said sternly. "She's released to my jurisdiction as commander of the military attachment to Shifter Bureau. Your CO has the orders," he told the sergeant.

Carly wondered if the CO—commanding officer—did. Walker couldn't have known what they would find here, couldn't have arranged this in advance. *Tiger* hadn't known until whatever bond between him and his cub had awakened.

Dylan hadn't said a word. He had a lot of

power, no matter that he was no longer a Shiftertown leader. But relinquishing the leader's duties to his son meant Dylan was at large, roaming around to take care of things. *Causing trouble,* Connor always said darkly.

Carly wondered if Dylan had known about this little hideout, if he'd known about the tiger-girl. If so, and if he'd kept it from Tiger, Carly was going to have a serious talk with him.

But no, Dylan wasn't the type to keep that kind of information to himself. He'd not only have told Tiger but arranged for a snatch and grab raid to rescue her. How Dylan had found them, though, Carly had no idea.

She'd worry about it later. For now, she was happy to slide her arm around Tiger. "Come on," she said. "Let's get her home and you fixed up."

"She'll need clothes," Connor pointed out. He looked down at himself and flinched. "Shite, so will I."

"Did ye shred your garments all over the place again?" Sean Morrissey asked. "I keep telling you about that, lad."

Sean was the Guardian of their Shiftertown —he was quieter than Liam, his role of sending

Shifters to the Summerland making him a little more contemplative.

Tiger didn't appear to hear any of them. He slowly released the tiger-girl without letting go of her completely, keeping her attention on him. One step at a time, he eased her toward the outer door.

The soldiers fidgeted, hands on weapons. Walker's men watched them carefully, their pistols ready as well. If one thing went wrong here, bullets would fly once more.

Carly let go of Tiger long enough to approach Liam. "Give her your shirt."

Liam stared at her. "Wha—?"

Dylan's lips twitched. "Do it, lad."

Liam heaved a sigh. "The things I sacrifice for the lot of you." He skimmed his T-shirt off over his head and handed it to Carly.

The shirt was big, tight on Liam, but would hang loose on the tiger-girl. Liam looked a bit embarrassed standing around with his chest hair out, and he folded his arms while Sean openly grinned.

Carly shook out the dust from the shirt and handed it to Tiger. "You'd better help her with this."

Tiger took the garment without looking at Carly. He brought the shirt between himself and his daughter and touched the cloth to her skin.

The tiger-girl jumped and hissed. Carly wondered if anyone had given her clothes before, if she even understood what they were.

The tiger-girl calmed a bit, leaned to the shirt, and took a big sniff. Her face screwed up and she snarled.

Connor laughed. "That's what she thinks of *you*, Uncle Liam."

The tiger-woman jerked her head up and switched her yellow gaze to Connor. She studied him a moment, and then her lips curved and she let out a hoarse, "Ha!"

"See, she agrees with me," Connor said, grinning hugely. "It's all right, lass. Uncle Liam can't help it. You'll get used to his scent in time."

Sean chuckled. Liam pretended to look annoyed, but Carly saw his concern for Tiger and the young woman. Liam might seem harsh at times, but he watched over all his Shifters with a fatherly eye, protecting them as he did his own family.

Tiger bunched up the shirt and lifted it so he

could slide it over the tiger-girl's head. She
yowled, backing up fast, almost into the
cage again.

"It's all right," Connor told her swiftly.
"Here, give it to me."

He took the shirt from Tiger's slack hands
and pulled it over his own head. Connor
smoothed it down over his torso and then
spread his hands. "See? Nothing to worry
about." He wrinkled his nose. "Though Uncle
Liam can be rank."

"Leave off, lad," Liam said good-humoredly.

Connor skimmed out of the T-shirt and
offered it to the tiger-woman.

She came forward again, step after hesitant
step. Carly held her breath. The entire room
watched, even the soldiers who'd fought them,
as the tiger-girl reached out and very carefully
touched the shirt.

Connor did nothing, only held the shirt still.
The girl drew her hand back, and then, her face
set, quickly snatched the T-shirt from Connor.

She held it in her fist a moment before she
tried to gather it up as Connor had, but it was
clear she'd never worn clothing before. She
didn't know what to do.

Connor reached to help her. The tiger-girl jerked away, her breath coming fast. She turned to Tiger, confused, and held out the shirt.

Carly could see Connor's hurt that she didn't trust him. He balled his fists but did and said nothing—he wasn't going to press the issue and maybe frighten her further.

Carly's heart went out to him. There would be time, she thought, time to get to know the tiger-girl, to learn what she'd been through, to teach her that they would take care of her. Time for her to grow used to them, to learn that Connor had a heart as big as Texas.

Carly pressed her fingertips to her lips as Tiger helped his cub get the shirt over her head. More confusion ensued as she struggled to shove her arms through the sleeves—she had to bash at them with her fists until her hands poked through.

At last Tiger got the shirt settled on her. As Carly had suspected, the fabric was long enough to cover the tiger-girl down to her thighs.

Without thinking, Carly reached over and pulled the tiger-girl's hair loose from the shirt's collar where it was caught. She'd have done the same for one of her sisters, for Kim, for Kim's little girl.

Instantly the tiger-girl swung around, ready to strike, but when her gaze connected with Carly's, she arrested the movement.

She locked eyes with Carly, her curled hand raised, like a cat who'd started to swat and then realized this might be a friend. Carly froze, careful not to move.

The tiger-girl stared at her for a long time, and then she reached out and ever so slowly brushed a fingertip over Carly's hair.

She blinked, wonder filling her expression. She drew her hand back and touched her own hair, her brows furrowing.

"Don't you worry about that," Carly said. "We'll give you a good wash and trim and fix you right up. You'll be the envy of everyone with that black and orange hair."

She thought of Seth, whose hair was the identical combination of colors, and her heart squeezed. She needed to get home.

Tiger laced his arm around his daughter. She clung to him as they moved, one step at a time, through the parting soldiers, watched over by Walker's men. Carly followed immediately behind Tiger, with Connor behind her. Sean and Liam came after them, Dylan bringing up the rear.

Slowly the procession moved to the next room and the next and next, and then up the stairs to the ground floor of the little house. It was dark when they stepped out onto the porch, disorienting Carly for a moment. It had been late afternoon when they'd arrived, and the sun had vanished in the meantime.

A wave of exhaustion hit her. Carly had been up since three a.m., and the long journey and lack of sleep was catching up to her.

The tiger-girl didn't flinch when Tiger took her out under the sky. This told Carly she'd been outside before, possibly while being moved from one prison to another—obviously she'd been brought here from Area 51 at some point in her life. Carly couldn't imagine her captors letting her out for any other reason.

The tiger-girl hissed when her bare feet touched the grating stones on the path, ones Carly could feel through her thin sandals. Tiger calmly lifted his daughter and carried her.

Carly hesitated a step, waiting for the tiger-girl to fight him, but she seemed to understand that Tiger had come to take care of her. The parent-cub bond had already been in place—it had just needed activation. The tiger-girl wrapped her arms around Tiger's neck and relaxed into him.

Tiger carried her down the path Carly had come up with Tyson, straight to a gray SUV that hadn't been there before. Carly didn't know whose it was, but Walker strode past and opened the doors.

Tiger climbed into the back and sat down with the tiger-girl on his lap. He jerked his head at Carly, indicating she should join them.

Carly hung back, not wanting to scare the young woman, but the tiger-girl only glanced at Carly and then rested her head on Tiger's shoulder. She was as exhausted as Carly.

Carly scrambled in, settling herself against Tiger, seeking his warmth.

Connor reached the SUV and peered under the seat Carly was sitting on. "Oi, those are *my* clothes." He snatched them out, staring at them in puzzlement. "Ones from home, I mean. How'd you know to bring them?" he asked Walker.

"I didn't." Walker jabbed his thumb at Sean. "His idea."

"Because I knew if you decided to shift ye wouldn't bother to strip down first, ye daft lad," Sean said. "Some in there for Tiger too."

"Wicked." Connor hugged the shirt and jeans to his chest. "I'm glad *you* picked them out, not Uncle Liam. The man has no taste."

"Hear you loud and clear, nephew." Liam looked into the SUV at Tiger. "What do you want to do, big guy?"

"Take her home," Tiger said without hesitation. "Where she belongs."

Liam chewed his lip, and Carly felt for him. This would be tricky. Tiger himself wasn't supposed to exist—his records had been erased when he'd been rescued from Area 51. He did covert ops for Shifter Bureau, yes, but only a few humans besides Walker knew about him. Bringing in yet another un-Collared Shifter, who happened to be Tiger's half-crazed daughter, would be difficult to hide.

But if anyone could do it, Liam and Dylan could, Carly thought with tired confidence. They'd worked major miracles for all their Shifters.

Liam squared his shoulders. "Right," he said, then took a step back and slammed the door.

Connor, dressed now, climbed into the front passenger seat and twisted to talk to them around its high back. "What's your name?" he asked the tiger-girl.

The tiger-girl looked at him blankly. Tiger hadn't had a name when he'd come to them, either. Carly had called him Tiger, and Tiger had decided that was his name.

"She'll pick her own," Carly said. "But no rush."

Walker slid into the driver's seat and shut the door, fitting his key into the ignition.

"Is this yours?" Carly asked in surprise. "I've never seen you drive it before."

"I use it for some ops," Walker answered as he adjusted the rearview mirror.

"How did you even know where to find us?" Carly continued. "Though I'm really glad you did."

Dylan, who'd approached Walker's window, answered her. "I have a GPS tracker on my truck. For when Connor decides to borrow it without asking."

Connor didn't look abashed. "Good thing, huh?"

The soldiers who'd guarded the tiger-girl were starting down the hill. They stayed behind Walker's men for now, but Carly bounced on her seat, worried.

"Can we get going, Walker, honey?" she asked.

Tiger-girl raised her head, catching Carly's anxiousness. She saw the men coming, and her eyes widened with fear. *"Apúrate!"* she shouted and then sent a string of words Carly didn't know at Walker.

"Well, shite," Connor said, his jaw slack. "She *can* talk."

The tiger-girl waved her hand at Walker, becoming more and more agitated as words came out of her mouth.

"Spanish," Carly said as Walker unhurriedly pulled out and headed back to the paved road. "Duh. Why were we thinking she'd only speak English?"

Tiger shrugged. "Because I do?"

"Makes sense though." Carly buckled her seatbelt. She contemplated explaining seat belts to the tiger-girl but gave up as the young woman sank into Tiger and closed her eyes. "Someone must have been feeding her and looking after her. If those people spoke Spanish, she'd have picked it up from them. All kids learn languages from listening to adults. If her caretakers had spoken Norwegian, she'd have learned Norwegian."

Carly felt rather proud of herself for the deduction. Connor beamed at her then swung around in his seat as Walker drove down the hill.

They passed Tyson's DPS car in which he'd driven Carly, then Dylan's truck not far behind it. Carly hoped Kirk would look after Tyson and that he wouldn't get into too much trouble. He was a nice guy.

Tiger began murmuring to the tiger-girl in Spanish. Carly spoke only a few words of that language, but Tiger adapted to languages faster than fast. If the young woman had spoken Icelandic, he'd even now be telling her everything would be all right in Icelandic.

The tiger-girl relaxed against him, and Carly started to relax as well, Tiger's voice soothing.

The long night, Carly's worry, shock, and fear, and the amazement and emotion of finding the tiger-girl crashed into her all at once. She still wasn't sure who all the soldiers had been or how they'd be taken care of, but she'd let Dylan and Sons fix all that. It was what they did. Right now, Walker was taking her, Tiger, Connor and the tiger-girl home.

Home—to Seth and the place Carly was happy.

To her mate's voice and presence and the

SUV's smooth movement on the winding roads, Carly fell asleep.

CHAPTER TEN

W hen Carly woke it was daybreak. She pulled herself up from where she'd slumped against Tiger to see that they'd slowed to drive through Austin's roads.

Tiger was dressed, wearing sweat pants and a T-shirt. Carly had no memory of him pulling on clothes, but she'd slept pretty hard, dreaming of tigers and cubs.

Tiger's daughter sat beside him, staring out at the passing city in both trepidation and curiosity.

The smell in the SUV wasn't good. The tiger-girl hadn't bathed since who the hell knew when, and the rest of them were getting rank as well. Carly tried to breathe through her mouth and anticipated a nice long bath with all her scented salts dumped in.

She'd show tiger-girl—they really needed to find out her name—what a great thing a sweet-smelling shower gel was, as well as lots of shampoo, conditioner, and maybe some restoring hair oils. That is, if they didn't have to cut her hair off and start again. Carly wondered how tiger-girl was going to feel about *that*.

Tiger's daughter. Carly shivered, but in a good way. Since Carly was Tiger's mate, the girl would be her stepdaughter. So what if she and the young woman were about the same age? Tiger was, strictly speaking, a lot older than Carly, as Shifters aged differently from humans. The tiger-girl would still be considered very young, a cub going through her Transition, the Shifter equivalent of puberty. Poor kid.

Walker, who looked as fresh and alert as he had when he'd entered the tiger-girl's prison, turned onto Shiftertown's main street.

The fact that all Shiftertowns were a hotbed of gossip was made clear by the fact that, despite the early hour, every Shifter was outside, on porches, in yards, and on sidewalks, to watch Walker drive by, followed by Dylan and his sons in his white pickup.

The SUV's windows were darkened, but that didn't stop every Shifter and the few humans who lived here from trying to peer inside. Carly saw Ronan holding up the polar bear cub, Olaf, so he could see over everyone else's head.

The tiger-girl stared out the window, hand against the glass. Her expression moved from fear, to eagerness, to fear again.

But she had courage. She'd been through hell, yet she'd decided to trust Tiger, and by extension Carly and Connor.

When the SUV pulled into the driveway of Liam's house, however, the tiger-girl's panic returned. Riding in a vehicle was one thing— she must have done this before, though perhaps not without being caged or chained. It wasn't the journey that had been bad for her, Carly realized, but the arrival at a new place, a new prison. She must be wondering what hellhole she'd be put into this time.

Connor hopped to the ground, coming around to open the back door from the outside. He handed Carly down, and then Tiger began to lift his daughter out.

Abruptly the tiger-girl shifted to her half-beast and fought him. Her keening pierced the fog in Carly's head, and Connor clapped his hands over his ears.

Walker simply got out of the SUV and stood next to it, hands in an at-ease position. No help at all.

"It's all right, sweetie," Carly yelled over the noise. "Um… *está bien*." She hoped that was right.

The tiger-girl clung to Tiger, her shrieks not decreasing in spite of Tiger speaking rapidly to her in Spanish.

Carly shook her head. "She'll have to learn we won't hurt her. Just don't let any of the Shifters tell you she should be locked up for her own good or something dumb-ass like that."

Tiger shot her a look over his struggling daughter's head. She saw in his eyes profound appreciation, gratitude for her understanding, and love.

Carly warmed under his gaze. She knew Tiger would never be able to express all he wanted to in words, so she simply smiled at him. "That's what mates are for, honey. Oh, it sounds like Seth is awake."

A cry came from the house, more of a bellow, really. Seth was a strong little boy, and he'd learned from day one how to use his lungs.

He was no doubt pissed off that he'd been left behind while Carly and Tiger ran off to have exciting adventures. Seth was only four months old, but he already knew how to make his feelings known. His yellow-eyed glare said it all.

He could also break into a huge smile and let out a baby squeal that pierced eardrums. Carly couldn't be prouder.

"Coming, my bundle of joy," she called up to the front door Kim had opened. Kim stepped out, holding a squirming and howling Seth. Carly's heart lightened as she dashed up the porch steps and swept her son into her arms.

Seth immediately quieted, except for a little "Bah!" as Carly held him close. She kissed his downy black and orange hair, her eyes growing moist in gratitude for this little gift.

She noticed it had gone silent behind her. The tiger-girl was standing beside Tiger, staring at Seth, no longer fighting. Her lips parted in wonder.

Connor, on the other hand, had his gaze on the tiger-girl. No one else was looking at him, so Carly caught him in an unguarded moment.

Hmm, Carly thought in immediate interest.

She's just starting her Transition, and his isn't far behind. Well, well. We shall see.

Carly held up Seth so the tiger-girl could see him. "Come on over here, sweetie, and meet your brother. Your, uh, *hermano*."

The tiger-girl blinked at the word, her stunned gaze still fixed on Seth. After a moment, she moved forward, very slowly, Tiger beside her. Carly jounced Seth, letting the tiger-girl see him while still protecting him.

The tiger-girl took the first step up the porch, then the next, and the next, halting when she reached Carly and Seth. The morning breeze swept away her raw scent, and her agitated breath was ragged in the stillness.

She stared down at Seth for a long time, then she reached out a careful finger and brushed a lock of his tiger-striped hair.

"Hermano?" she whispered.

"Yep," Carly said, her voice quiet. "Brother."

Seth reached both tiny hands to the tiger-girl, burst into a big grin, and said, "Wheeezzthp!"

Tiger-girl's voice went even softer. *"Hermana,"* she said to Seth. Then her face screwed up, and she burst into tears.

AFTER DARK THAT NIGHT, TIGER GAZED DOWN at his daughter where she slept in the bedroom that had been Sean Morrissey's once up on a time.

She was clean, bathed by Carly in a ceremony that had seemed to last a very long time and consisted of splashing, shrieks, laughter, crying, and more laughter. Carly hadn't let Tiger into the bathroom, so he'd hovered worriedly outside it, joined by Connor, who looked equally as concerned.

When the two women had emerged, both had been soaked, but the tiger-girl had been dressed in a thick robe, her hair clean if not completely untangled. Tiger remembered how awful his own hair had been after his captivity— Liam had handed him a full bottle of shampoo and told him to use all of it.

Carly had been very wet, but her look was one of triumph and pride. Tiger's daughter had valiantly stayed awake to be dressed in clothes borrowed from Sean's mate Andrea, who was about the same size, and then they'd gone downstairs to eat. Tiger-girl had grabbed everything with her hands and stuffed it into her mouth, eating whatever she could reach. Kim and Liam looked worried, but Carly had only smiled and said they needed patience.

The tiger-girl had fallen asleep once she'd finished eating, climbing out of the chair they'd had to show her how to use, and lying down on the floor. Tiger had lifted her and carried her to bed.

"My cub," he whispered.

All those years ago, he'd thought he'd lost her. The pain of that had been unbearable.

Now she was here, in his house, well out of reach of the soldiers and researchers who'd held her captive. She'd told him bits and pieces on the way home, but while she could speak, the number of words she knew was limited and she didn't know how to explain things. Plus, as Tiger remembered from his own long captivity, it was likely she didn't know who the people who'd held her were and what all they'd done to her.

Tiger would find out. He'd hunt down her captors her and explain a few things to them.

Walker had already told him some of it. The soldiers guarding his daughter had been tasked with keeping her hidden at all costs, especially from Tiger. Tiger needed to ferret out the details, but apparently the researchers who had taken his cub from the Area 51 compound so many years ago had been studying her and trying to decide how to make a weapon of her ever since.

A few soldiers had been watching Shiftertown since Tiger had come here, keeping an eye on him. Their watchfulness had increased as soon as the tiger-girl had gone into her Transition. The watchers had seen Tiger leaving Shiftertown and had followed, calling ahead to the men already at the compound, and putting backup on standby.

Walker thought they might be a secret branch of Shifter Bureau—kind of a dark ops troop, but he wasn't sure. He and Dylan were digging to find out.

Dylan's trackers had alerted him that something was going on when they saw Tiger followed from the outskirts of Shiftertown. Dylan turned on the tracker for his pickup and called Walker, saying Tiger was going to need backup. It had taken Walker an hour or so to put together a rescue mission, and they'd headed out after Tiger.

Tiger was sure that his daughter's budding Transition had triggered the search-and-rescue instinct in his brain. He'd never felt a pull so strongly before, one it would have killed him to ignore.

The compulsion made sense now. His cub had been calling out to her father, and the father in Tiger had responded.

He'd deal with those who'd kept her from him. Meanwhile, he'd make his daughter part of the family, teach her, raise her, help her through her Transition. For now, she was here, and safe, and that was enough.

He sensed Carly approach before she slid her hand into his. "She's beautiful, Tiger."

She was. Tiger had a son and now a daughter, and the mate of his heart stood by his side. No one in the world could be as lucky.

"We'll take care of her," Carly said.

Unnecessary words. Of course they'd take care of her. But Carly liked to spell everything out. She liked to talk, and Tiger enjoyed listening to her. Carly's voice could take him out of the pain that had once surrounded him, giving him peace, happiness.

"Come on to bed," she said, her touch sending warmth through him. "I finally got Seth down. I know he's probably too young to understand what's going on, but I think he does anyway. You saw how he liked her right away.

He doesn't usually respond to people that quickly."

"He knows," Tiger said, sure of it.

Carly tugged at him. "Kim and Liam said they'd check on her. And Connor. Connor seems very taken with her." She grinned as though delighted about something.

Yes, Connor had been helpful, Tiger thought, turning away with Carly. And his daughter had responded to Connor, far more easily than she had to anyone else except him and Carly.

Tiger halted, his eyes narrowing, and he let out a growl.

Carly laughed, the sound quiet. "We can worry about that later. For now, let's go sleep in a soft bed and cuddle up."

Tiger agreed. There'd be time, lots of time, if Tiger had anything to say about it.

He kept hold of Carly's hand and let her tow him up the stairs. They went to the bedroom they shared at the top of the house, moonlight filling the room. The door to the cubbyhole where Seth slept was closed, but Tiger knew his son was there and well, even without the baby monitor Carly kept on the dresser, knew every intake of his breath.

Carly stretched and moved toward the bed, letting her robe fall as she went. She wore one of the very short, flimsy nighties she liked. They were so thin Tiger wondered why she bothered with them at all.

Not that Tiger minded seeing her curved body pressing the wispy fabric. His heart beat faster, and he closed the door.

"Carly," he said.

She turned. "Hmm?"

"I love you."

Carly had been at his side every step of the way on this journey, had helped him find his cub, had helped save her. All without a word of complaint.

More than that, she was simply Carly, the beautiful woman who'd made him whole again.

Carly smiled. "I love you too, big guy. You know that."

Knowing and hearing her say it were two different things. Tiger loved how the words sounded as they came out of her mouth.

In another moment he was kissing the lips that formed the words, his hands finding the warm flesh beneath the gauzy fabric. Carly laughed into his kiss, gathering him close as they went down on the bed.

Tiger's hands made short work of the nighty, and then he was coming down on her, Carly welcoming him.

"Love you so much," he said as he slid inside her, her face softening as she began to feel him.

"Love you." Carly's words became a groan. She cupped his face and looked straight into his eyes as he rocked into her for his first thrust. *"Mate of my heart."*

AUTHOR'S NOTE

Thank you for reading! I originally wrote *Tiger Striped* to be included in a boxed set with about 30 other authors, but the set was cancelled right when I was ready to turn in the story. Oh well, I said, and sent it off for another proofread in preparation to release it myself.

Events in *Tiger Striped* occur after *Midnight Wolf*, which is Book 11 of the full-length Shifters Unbound novels (or entry #20 if we count everything in the series).

Shifters Unbound will continue! I am publishing the full-length books myself now, and they will be available in print (online and special order in bookstores), e-book (from all booksellers), and in audio (Audible and iTunes).

I have more to say about this world, and many characters who need stories, including Ben; Peigi and Reid; the bear Shifters of Las Vegas and North Carolina (see *Mate Bond*); Connor of course; and many others, plus I'd like to do a full-length book about Dylan.

You can stay up to date about the series by signing up for my newsletter (if you have not already), via my website:

http://www.jenniferashley.com

Enter your name and email address in the form at the top, and you'll receive the email when books are ready for pre-order or have been released.

Thank you for being a Shifters Unbound fan. We have more to do before we're done!

All my best,
  Jennifer Ashley

ABOUT THE AUTHOR

New York Times bestselling and award-winning author Jennifer Ashley has written more than 85 published novels and novellas in romance, urban fantasy, and mystery under the names Jennifer Ashley, Allyson James, and Ashley Gardner. Her books have been nominated for and won Romance Writers of America's RITA (given for the best romance novels and novellas of the year), several *RT BookReviews* Reviewers Choice awards (including Best Urban Fantasy, Best Historical Mystery, and Career Achievement in Historical Romance), and Prism awards for her paranormal romances. Jennifer's books have been translated into more than a dozen languages and have earned starred reviews in *Booklist*.

More about the Jennifer's books can be found at

http://www.jenniferashley.com

CPSIA information can be obtained
at www.ICGtesting.com
Printed in the USA
LVHW021319271218
601883LV00001BA/6